Revenge.

As Nikos strode down the hall towards the east wing of the house he smiled grimly, remembering the way Anna had melted into his arms. The bewildered look in her eyes after he'd pulled away. She was putty in his hands. Like the old song promised, that single kiss had told him everything he needed to know.

She still wanted him.

She still cared for him.

That was her weakness.

His son was all that mattered now. He was the one who needed Nikos's protection…and love.

Dear Reader

This is a very special book for me. I first had the idea for this story when my daughter was four months old; I got the magical call that I'd sold the book when I was seven months pregnant with my son.

Like anything worthwhile, becoming a writer wasn't easy. I wrote for seven years as an unpublished author and wondered if I'd ever get that call. But, just like when you fall in love with the right man after years of dating the wrong ones, it can only take one instant for a person's whole world to change.

In Anna's case, her world changes when her billionaire boss shows up at her house one rainy night. She's secretly loved the ruthless tycoon for years, but if she'd known what would happen she might never have opened up her arms—and her bed. They conceive a child, but right before the baby is due she learns a devastating secret that nearly destroys her.

She runs away to Russia, intending to raise her son alone. But Nikos tracks her down, determined to punish her for stealing his infant son like a thief in the night. Poor as she is, she has a royal bloodline, and refuses to submit to the tyrant who betrayed her; while he, in revenge for her disloyalty, intends to possess her—both as his bride and in his bed.

I hope you enjoy reading Anna and Nikos's story as much as I loved writing it. They say a woman never forgets her first time, and this is mine.

If you'd like to learn more about me or my books, please visit me at www.jennielucas.com. I'd love to hear from you.

Jennie Lucas

THE GREEK BILLIONAIRE'S BABY REVENGE

BY
JENNIE LUCAS

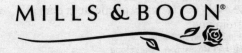

MILLS & BOON®

First published in Great Britain 2007
Harlequin Mills & Boon Limited,
Eton House, 18-24 Paradise Road, Richmond, Surrey TW9 1SR

© Jennie Lucas 2007

ISBN-13: 978 0 263 85347 6

Set in Times Roman 10½ on 13¼ pt
01-0807-44583

Printed and bound in Spain
by Litografia Rosés, S.A., Barcelona

Jennie Lucas grew up dreaming about faraway lands. At fifteen, hungry for experience beyond the borders of her small Idaho city, she went to a Connecticut boarding school on scholarship. She took her first solo trip to Europe at sixteen, then put off college and travelled around the US, supporting herself with jobs as diverse as petrol station cashier and newspaper advertising assistant.

At twenty-two, she met the man who would be her husband. After their marriage, she graduated from Kent State with a degree in English. Seven years after she started writing she got the magical call from London that turned her into a published author.

Since then life has been hectic, with a new writing career and a sexy husband and two babies under two, but she's having a wonderful (albeit sleepless) time. She loves immersing herself in dramatic, glamorous, passionate stories. Maybe she can't physically travel to Morocco or Spain right now, but for a few hours a day, while her children are sleeping, she can be there in her books.

Jennie loves to hear from her readers. You can visit her website at www.jennielucas.com or drop her a note at jennie@jennielucas.com

To Pete, the sexiest, smartest and best.
Every day, I love you more.

CHAPTER ONE

Snow was falling so hard and fast that she could barely see through the windshield.

Anna Rostoff parked her old car in the front courtyard of the palace, near the crumbling stone fountain, and pulled on the brake. Her hands shook as she peeled them from the steering wheel. She'd nearly driven off the road twice in the storm, but she had the groceries and, more importantly, the medicine for her baby's fever.

Taking a deep breath, she hefted the bag with one arm and climbed out into the night.

Cold air stung her cheeks as she padded through soft snow and ascended sweeping steps to the gilded double doors of the two-hundred-year-old palace. They were conserving electricity in favor of paying for food and diapers, so the windows were dark. Only a bare thread of moonlight illuminated the dark Russian forest.

We're going to make it, Anna thought. It was April, and spring still seemed like a forlorn dream, but they had candles and a shed full of wood. Once she found work as a translator she'd be able to make a new life with her four-month-old baby and her young sister. After months of hell, things were finally looking up.

She lifted her keys to the door.

Her eyes went wide as a chill descended her spine. The front door was open.

Barely able to breathe, she pushed into the grand foyer. In the shadows above, an ancient, unseen chandelier chimed discordantly as whirling flurries of snow came in from behind, whipped by a cold north wind.

"Natalie?" Anna's voice echoed down the hall.

In response, she heard a muffled scream.

She dropped the groceries. Potatoes tumbled out across the floor as she ran down the hall. Gasping, she shoved open the door into the back apartment.

A figure stood near the ceramic tile fireplace, his broad-shouldered form silhouetted darkly in the candlelight.

Nikos!

For one split second Anna's heart soared in spite of everything. Then she saw the empty crib.

"They took the baby, Anna," Natalie cried, her eyes owlish with fear behind her glasses. Two grim bodyguards, ruddy and devilish in the crackling firelight, flanked her sister on either side. She tried to leap from the high-backed chair, but one of Nikos's men restrained her. "They came in while I was dozing and snatched him from his crib. I heard him cry out and tried to stop them—"

Misha. Oh, God, her son. Where was he? Held by some vicious henchman in the dark forest? Already spirited out of Russia to God knew where? Anna trembled all over. Her baby. Her sweet baby. Sick with desperation and fear, she turned to face the monster she'd once loved.

Nikos's expression was stark, almost savage. The man who'd laughed with her in New York and Las Vegas, drinking ouzo and singing in Greek, had disappeared. In his place was a man without mercy. Even in the dim light she could see that. Olive-skinned and black-haired, he was as handsome as ever, but something had changed.

The crooked nose he'd broken in a childhood fight had once been the only imperfection in classic good looks. Now his face had an edge of fury—of cruelty. He'd always been strong, but there were hard planes to his body that hadn't been there before. His shoulders were somehow broader, his arms wider, as if he'd spent the last four months beating his opponents to a pulp in the boxing ring. His cheekbones were razor-sharp, his arms thick with muscle, his blue eyes limitless and cold. Looking into his eyes was like staring into a half-frozen sea.

Once she'd loved him desperately; now she hated him, this man who had betrayed her. This man who, with kisses and sweet words whispered against her skin at night, had convinced her to betray herself.

"Hello, Anna." Nikos's voice was deep, dangerous, tightly controlled.

She rushed at him, grabbing the lapels of his black cashmere coat. "What have you done with my baby?" She tried to shake him, pounded on his chest. *"Where is he?"*

He grabbed her wrists. "He is no longer your concern."

"Give me my child!"

"No." His grip was grim, implacable.

She struggled in his arms. Once his touch had set her body aflame. No longer. Not now that she knew what kind of man he really was.

"Misha!" she shrieked helplessly.

Nikos's grasp tightened as he pulled her closer, preventing her from thrashing her arms or clawing his face. "*My son* belongs with me."

It was exactly what she'd known he'd say, but Anna still staggered as if he had hit her. This time Nikos let her go. She grabbed the rough edge of the long wooden table to keep herself from sliding to the floor. She had to be strong—strong for her baby. She had to think of a way to save her son.

In spite of her best efforts, a tear left a cold trail down her cheek. Wiping it away furiously, she raised her chin and glared at Nikos with every ounce of hate she possessed. "You can't do this!"

"I can and I will. You lost the right to be his mother when you stole him away like a thief in the night."

Anna brought her hands to her mouth, knowing Nikos could use his money and power and man-eating lawyers to keep her from her son forever. She'd been stupid to run away, and now her worst nightmare had come true. Her baby would grow up without her, living in Las Vegas with a heartless, womanizing billionaire and his new mistress…

"I'm so sorry, Anna," Natalie sobbed behind her. "I tried to stop them. I tried."

"It's all right, Natalie," Anna whispered. But it wasn't all right. It would never be all right again.

A door slammed back against the wall, causing Anna to jump as a third bodyguard entered from the kitchen and placed a tray on the table. Steam rose from the samovar as Nikos went to the table and poured undiluted tea, followed by hot water, into a blue china cup.

She stared at her great-grandmother's china teacup. It looked so fragile and small in his fingers, she thought. It could be crushed in a moment by those tanned, muscular hands.

Nikos could destroy anything he wanted. And he had.

"I've been here two weeks," Anna said bitterly as she watched him take a drink. "What took you so long?"

He lowered the cup, and his unsmiling gaze never once looked from hers.

"I ordered my men to wait until you and the child were separated. Easier that way. Less risk of you doing something foolish."

Stupid. Stupid. She never should have left her baby— not even to go to an all-night market in St. Petersburg. After all, Misha wasn't really sick, just teething and cranky, with a tiny fever that barely registered on her thermometer.

"I was stupid to leave," she whispered.

"It took you four months to figure that out?"

Anna barely heard him. No, the really stupid move had been coming here in the first place. After four months on the move, always just one step ahead of Nikos's men, and with money running out, Anna had convinced herself that Nikos wouldn't be staking out her great-grandmother's old palace. Now mortgaged to the hilt, the crumbling palace was their family's last asset. Natalie was trying to repair the murals in hopes that they'd be able to find a buyer and pay off their paralyzing debt. A fruitless hope, in Anna's opinion.

As fruitless as trying to escape Nikos Stavrakis. He was bigger than her by six inches, and eighty pounds of hard muscle. He had three bodyguards, with more waiting in cars hidden behind the palace.

The police, she thought, but that hope faded as soon as it came. By the time she managed to summon a policeman Nikos would be long gone. Or he'd pay off anyone who took her side. Nikos Stavrakis's wealth and power made him above the law.

She had only one option left. Begging.

"Please," she whispered. She took a deep breath and forced herself to say in a louder voice, "Nikos, please don't take my child. It would kill me."

He barked a harsh laugh. "That's what I'd call a bonus."

She should have known better than to ask him for anything. "You…you heartless bastard!"

"Heartless?" He threw the cup at the fireplace. It smashed and fell in a thousand chiming pieces. "Heartless!" he roared.

Suddenly afraid, Anna drew back. "Nikos—"

"You let me believe that my son was dead! I thought you both were dead. I returned from New York and you were gone. Do you know how many days I waited for the ransom note, Anna? Do you have any idea how long I waited for your bodies to be discovered? Seven days. You made me wait seven damn days before you bothered to let me know you were both alive!"

Anna's breaths came in tiny rattling gasps. "You betrayed me. You caused my father's death! Did you think I'd never find out?"

His dark eyes widened, then narrowed. "Your father made his own choices, as you have made yours. I'm taking my son back where he belongs."

"No. Please." Tears welled up in her eyes and she grabbed at his coat sleeve. "You can't take him. I'm— I'm still breastfeeding. Think what it would do to Misha to lose his mother, the only parent he's ever known…"

His eyes went dark, and Anna wanted to bite off her tongue. How could she have drawn attention to the fact that she'd not only denied Nikos the chance to experience the first four months of their child's life, but she'd broken her promise about their son's name?

Then he bared his teeth in the wolflike semblance of a smile. "You are mistaken, *zoe mou*. I have no intention of taking him away from you."

She was so overwhelmed that she nearly embraced him. "Thank you—oh, God, thank you. I really thought…"

He took a step closer, towering over her. "Because I'm taking you as well."

He should have savored this moment.

Instead, Nikos was furious. For four months he'd fantasized about taking vengeance on Anna. *No, not vengeance*, he corrected himself. *Justice.*

Some justice. His lip curled into a half-snarl.
Bringing Anna back to Las Vegas, where he'd see her
face across his table every day? That was the last thing
he wanted.

He'd intended to take his son and leave, as she
deserved. But from the moment he'd first seen his baby
son a surge of love had risen in him that he'd never felt
before. At that moment he'd known he could never
allow his son to be hurt. He'd kill anyone who tried.

For four months he'd hated Anna. But now…

Hurting her would hurt his son. His child needed his
mother. The two were bonded.

The payback was off.

He cursed under his breath, narrowing his eyes.

Anna had lost all her pregnancy weight, and then
some. Under her coat's frayed edges he could see the
swell of her breasts beneath her tight sweater, see the
curve of her slender hips in the worn, slim-fitting jeans.
There were hungry smudges beneath her cheekbones
that hadn't been there before, and tiny worry lines
around her blue-green eyes. The tightly controlled secretary was gone. Her long dark hair, which she'd always
pulled back in a tight bun, now fell wild around her
shoulders. It was…sexy.

Anna slowly exhaled and stared up at him, her eyes
pleading for mercy. Even now, she was the most beautiful woman he'd ever seen. Her aristocratic heritage
showed in the perfect bone structure of her heart-shaped
face, and in every move she made.

Once he'd been grateful for her skills. He'd admired

her dignity, her grace. He'd known Anna's value. As his executive secretary, she'd run interference with government officials, employees, vendors and investors, making decisions in his name. She'd reflected well both upon him and the brand of luxury hotels he'd created around the world. Even now he still missed her presence in his office—the cool, precise secretary who'd made his business run so smoothly. She'd made it look easy.

It made him regret that he'd ever slept with her.

It made him furious that he was still so attracted to her.

Misha, indeed. A Russian nickname for Michael? Anna had promised to name their son after Nikos's maternal grandfather, but it didn't surprise him that she'd gone back on her word. She was a liar, just like her father.

"I had Cooper pack your things," he bit out. "We're leaving."

"But the storm—"

"We have snow chains and local drivers. The storm won't slow us down."

Anna glanced from Nikos to the empty crib, and the fight went out of her. Her shoulders sagged.

"You win. I'll go back with you," she said quietly.

Of course he'd won. He always won. Although this victory had come harder than he'd ever imagined, at a price he hadn't wanted. Already sick of the sight of her, he growled, "Let's go."

But as he turned away Anna's throaty voice said, "What about Natalie? I can't leave her here. She has to come with us."

"What?" her sister gasped.

Nikos whirled back with a snarl on his lips, incredulous that Anna was actually trying to dictate the terms of her surrender. Another Rostoff woman in his house? "No."

"No way, Anna!" Her sister echoed, pushing up her glasses. "I'm not going anywhere with him. Not after what he did to our father. Forget it!"

Anna ignored her. "Look around, Nikos. There's no money. I was planning to get a job as a translator to support us. I can't just leave her."

"I'm twenty-two! I can take care of myself!"

Anna whirled around to face her young sister. "You barely speak Russian, and all you know about is art. Mother doesn't have any more money to send you, and neither do I. What do you expect to eat? Paintbrushes?"

The girl's eyes filled with tears. "Maybe if we went to Vitya he would…"

"No!" Anna shouted.

Who was Vitya? Nikos wondered. Another impoverished aristocrat like Anna's father had been? For most of Anna's young life he'd forced his family to live off the charity of wealthy friends. She'd once dryly commented that that was how she'd learned to speak fluent French, Russian, Spanish and Italian—begging the Marquis de Savoie and Contessa di Ferazza for book money.

Although of course that had been before Alexander Rostoff had realized it would be simpler to just embezzle the money.

Aristocrats, he thought scornfully. Rather than live in the comforts of Nikos's house near Las Vegas, his brownstone in New York, or his villa in Santorini, Anna had kidnapped his baby son and moved from one cheap apartment to another.

His lip curled as he looked around the room. The back of the palace had been turned into a cheerless Soviet-era apartment. It was a little disorienting to be smack in the real thing, especially since Anna seemed to be using nineteenth-century standards to light and heat the room.

"How could you force my son to live like this?" he abruptly demanded. "What kind of mother are you?"

Anna's turquoise eyes widened as she gripped the gilded edge of a high-backed chair. "I kept him warm and safe—"

"Warm?" Incredulously, he looked at the single inadequate fireplace, the flickering candles on the wooden table, the frost lining the inside of the window. "Safe?"

Anna flinched. "I did the best I could."

Nikos shook his head with a derisive snort as Cooper, his right-hand man and director of security, entered the room. He gave Nikos a nod.

Nikos made a show of glancing at his sleek platinum watch. "Your things are packed in the truck. Are you coming, or should we toss your suitcases in the snow?"

"We just need a minute for Natalie to pack her things—"

"Perhaps I have not made myself clear? There is no way in hell that I'm taking your sister with us. You're lucky I'm bringing you."

Anna folded her arms, thrusting up her chin. He knew

that expression all too well. She was ready to be stubborn, to fight, to prolong this argument until he had to drag her out of this place by her fingernails.

"Stay, then." He turned to leave, motioning for Cooper and his bodyguards to follow. "Feel free to visit our son next Christmas."

Precisely as he'd expected, Anna grabbed his arm.

"Wait. I'm coming with you. You know I am. But I can't just abandon Natalie."

He tried to shake off her grip, but she wouldn't let go. He looked into those beautiful blue-green eyes, wet with unshed tears. What was it about women and tears? How were they able to instantly manufacture them to get what they wanted? Well, it wouldn't work on him. He wouldn't be manipulated in this way. He wouldn't let her…

"You might have to go with him, Anna," Natalie said defiantly. "But I don't. I'm staying."

Nikos glanced at Anna's sister. The girl had fought like a crazed harpy to protect her nephew. Now, she just looked heartbreakingly young.

Something like guilt went through him. Angrily, he pushed it aside. If the Rostoffs were penniless, it wasn't his fault. As his secretary, Anna had been paid a six-figure salary for the last five years—enough to support her whole family in decent comfort.

So where had that money gone? He'd never seen Anna splurge on clothes or jewelry or cars. She bought things that were simple and well made but, unlike his current secretary, she avoided flashy luxury.

Anna's sister didn't look terribly royal either. In her

bulky sweatsuit, covered by an artist's smock, she stood by the frost-lined window with a bowed head. She was staring wistfully at the broken pieces of the blue china teacup he'd smashed against the fireplace.

His jaw tightened.

He gestured to Cooper, who instantly came forward. "Yes?"

"See that the girl has all the money and assistance she requires to live here or return to New York, as she wishes." In a lower voice, he added, "And find a replacement for that damn cup. At any price."

Cooper gave a single efficient nod. Nikos turned to Anna. "Satisfied?"

Anna raised her chin. Even now, when he'd given her far more than she deserved, she was defiant. "But how do I know you'll keep your word?"

That one small question made fury rise tight against his throat. He always kept his word. Always. And yet she dared insinuate that he was the one who was untrustworthy. After her father had stolen his money. After she herself had stolen his child.

He hated her so much at that moment he almost *did* leave her behind. He wanted to do it. But not at the cost of hurting his son. Damn her.

Gritting his teeth, he said, "Call your sister when we reach Las Vegas. You'll see I've kept my word."

"Very well." Anna's face was pale as she knelt beside her sister. "You'll accept his help, won't you, Natalie? Please."

The girl hesitated, and for a moment Nikos thought she

would refuse. Then her expression hardened. "All right. Since he's only paying back what he took from Father."

What the hell had Anna told her? Surrounded by bodyguards, he didn't have the time or inclination to find out. He'd tried to spare Anna the truth about her father, but he was done coddling her. It was time she knew the kind of man he really was. He would enjoy telling her.

And more than that, Nikos promised himself as they left the palace. Once they'd returned to his own private fiefdom in Las Vegas he would make her pay for her crimes. In private. In ways she couldn't even imagine.

Oh, yes, he promised himself grimly. She'd pay.

CHAPTER TWO

RIDING in the limo from the Las Vegas airport to Nikos's desert estate twenty miles outside the city gave Anna an odd sense of unreality.

In one long night she'd left darkness and winter behind. But it wasn't just the bright morning light that threw her. It wasn't just the harsh blue sky, or the dried sagebrush tumbling across the long private road, or the feel of the hot Nevada sun on her face.

It was the fact that nothing had changed. And yet everything had changed.

"Hello, miss," the housekeeper said as they entered the grand foyer.

"Welcome back, miss," a maid said, smiling shyly at the baby in Anna's arms.

The moment their limo had arrived inside the guarded gate the house steward and a small army of assistants had descended upon Nikos. He walked ahead with them now, signing papers and giving orders as he led them through the luxurious fortress he called a home. Members of his house staff had already spirited away her luggage.

Where had they taken it? Anna wondered. A guest-room? A dungeon?

Nikos's bedroom?

She shivered at the thought. No, surely not his bedroom. But for most of her pregnancy his room had been her home. She'd slept naked in his arms on hot summer nights. She'd caressed his body and kissed him with her heart on her lips. She'd dreamed of wearing his engagement ring and prayed to God that it would last. She'd been so sure that if he left her she would die.

But in the end she'd been the one who left.

Because the moment he'd found out she was pregnant he'd fired her. She'd gone from being his powerful, trusted assistant to a prisoner in this gilded cage. He'd ordered her to take her leisure, practically forcing her into bedrest, although she'd had a normal, healthy pregnancy.

Nikos had taken the job she loved and given it to a young, gorgeous blonde with no secretarial skills. He'd ordered the household staff to block the calls of her mother and sister. Then, during her final trimester, he'd suddenly refused to touch her. He'd abandoned her to go and stay, with his secretary Lindsey on hand, at the newly finished penthouse at L'Hermitage Casino Resort.

That should have been enough to make Anna leave him. That should have been more than enough. But it hadn't been until she'd found those papers showing that Nikos had deliberately destroyed her father's textiles company that she'd finally been fed up. Anna's hands tightened. Running away had been an act of self-defense for her and her child.

But now they were back. As Anna entered a wide gallery lined with old portraits, she could smell the flowers of the high desert. Spring was swift in southern Nevada, sometimes lasting only weeks. Wind and light cascaded through high open windows, oscillating the curtains. Her footsteps echoed in the wide hall as she followed Nikos and his men.

But a woman was with them, too: the perfect blonde who'd replaced Anna in Nikos's office, and in his bed. Anna watched Lindsey lean forward eagerly, touching his arm. She blinked, surprised at how much it hurt to see them together.

Nikos was impeccably gorgeous, as always. He'd showered and changed on the plane, and now wore dark designer slacks and a crisp white shirt that showed off his tanned olive skin. It wasn't just his height that made him stand out from the rest of his men, but his aura of power, worn as casually as his shirt.

Nikos had always stood out for her. Even now, looking at him, Anna felt her heart ache. It was too easy to remember the years they'd spent working together. In spite of his arrogance, she'd admired him. He'd seemed so straightforward and honest, so different from her former employer, Victor. Plus, Nikos had never tried to make a pass at her. For five years he'd taken time not just to teach her about the business, but also to rely upon her advice. At least until that night thirteen months ago when he'd shown up wild-eyed on her doorstep, and everything had changed between them forever.

But her job had meant everything to her. For the first

time in her life she'd felt strong. Capable. Valued. Was it any wonder that, even knowing her boss was a playboy, she'd fallen so totally under his spell?

As if he felt her gaze, Nikos glanced back to where she trailed behind with the baby. His eyes were dark, and a shiver went through her.

"He hates you, you know."

Anna glanced up at Lindsey, who was standing next to her. She had a scowl on her pouting pink lips, though she looked chic in a dark pinstriped suit with a tucked-in waist and miniskirt. Her tanned legs stretched forever into impossibly high heels.

Anna felt dowdy in comparison, wearing the same T-shirt and jeans from last night, with a sweater tied around her waist. Her hair, which hadn't been washed or combed since yesterday, was pulled back in a ponytail. She'd been afraid to leave her baby alone on the plane, even for the few minutes it would have taken to shower.

Next to Lindsey, Anna felt a million years old, worn out from running away, working odd jobs, trying to get by, raising her child. Lindsey was fresh and young, glossy and free. No wonder Nikos preferred her. The thought stung, even though she told herself that it didn't hurt.

"I don't care if he hates me." Anna nervously twisted her great-grandmother's wedding ring around her finger, fiddling with its bent-back tines and empty setting. She couldn't let Lindsey know how vulnerable she felt on the inside, how scared she was that the younger woman would soon take everything Anna cared about. She already had Nikos and her job. Would Misha be next?

Lindsey lifted a perfectly groomed eyebrow in disbelief. "You really think you've gotten away with it, don't you? You actually think Nikos will take you back."

Anna smoothed back a tuft of Misha's dark hair. "I don't want to be taken back. I'm here for my son. Nikos can rot in hell for all I care."

The girl gave Misha a crocodile smile that made Anna's skin crawl. "Yeah, right. As if anyone would believe that." Her perfectly made-up eyes narrowed. "But Nikos doesn't want you. He's got me now, and I keep him very satisfied, trust me. We'll be getting married soon."

Anna couldn't keep herself from glancing at Lindsey's left hand. It was bare. Remembering Nikos's wandering eye when she'd been just his secretary, Anna almost felt sorry for the girl. "Has he proposed?"

"No, but he—"

"Then you're kidding yourself," she said. "He'll never propose to you or anyone else. He's not the marrying kind."

Grinding her white teeth, Lindsey stopped in the hallway, and grabbed Anna's wrist. Her long acrylic nails bit into Anna's skin.

"Listen to me, you little bitch," Lindsey said softly. "Nikos is mine. Don't think for a second you can come back with your little brat and—"

Nikos spoke from behind her. "This is cozy. Catching up on office gossip?"

Lindsey whirled around, spots of hot color on her cheeks. "We…uh, that is…"

Anna hid a smile. But her pleasure at the blonde's discomfiture was short-lived as Nikos turned to her, reaching for the diaper bag on her shoulder.

"I need this."

"What? Why?" Anna stammered. The diaper bag held her whole life. Bought at a secondhand shop, it was overflowing with documents, diapers, wipes and snacks. It was the one item that Anna had taken with her every-where since Misha's birth.

"For my son." As he took the bag, he brushed her shoulder carelessly with his hand. An electric shock re-verberated across her body. For a single second it stopped her heart.

Then she realized that Nikos was taking Misha away from her.

And handing both bag and baby to her replacement.

"No!" Anna cried out, shaking herself out of her stupor. "Not to *her*!"

Nikos stared straight back at her, as if he were marking her over the barrel of a gun. "Good. Fight me. Give me a reason to throw you out of my house. I'm begging you."

Anna opened her mouth. And closed it.

"I thought so." He turned back to Lindsey. "Take my son to the nursery. I'll follow in a moment."

She tossed Anna a look of venomous triumph. "With pleasure."

As they passed him, Nikos kissed the baby on the forehead. "Welcome home, my son," he said tenderly.

Anna watched as Lindsey disappeared down the hall toward the nursery. She could see her baby's sweet little head bobble dangerously with every swaying step and clackety-clack of the girl's four-inch heels against the marble floor. She wondered if Nikos had destroyed all of Natalie's hand-painted murals and her own carefully chosen antique baby furniture. *He probably ordered Lindsey to redecorate the nursery from a catalog*, she thought, and her heart broke a little more.

As much as she'd hated being on the run, this was worse. Here, every hallway, every corner, held a memory of the past. Even looking at Nikos was a cruel reminder of the man she'd once thought him to be, the man she'd respected, the man she'd loved. That was the cruelest trick of all.

"You don't like Lindsey, do you?" Nikos said, watching her.

"No."

"Why?"

Did he want her to spell it out? To admit that she still had feelings for him in spite of everything he'd done? Not in this lifetime.

"I told you. After you fired me, I got calls at the house from vendors and managers at the worksite, complaining about her cutting off half your calls and screwing up your messages. Her mistakes probably cost the company thousands of dollars. It nearly caused a delay in the liquor license."

Nikos pressed his lips together, looking tense. "But you said those complaints stopped."

"Yes," she retorted. "When you had the house staff block all my calls. Even from my mother and sister!"

"That was for your own good. The calls were causing you stress. It was bad for the baby."

"My mother and sister needed me. My father had just died!"

"Your mother and sister need to stand on their own feet and learn to solve their own problems, rather than always running to you first. You had a new family to care for."

She squared her shoulders. She wasn't going to get into that old argument with him again. "And now you have a new secretary to care for you. How's she doing at solving all your problems? Has she even learned how to type?"

His jaw clenched, but he said only, "You seem very worried about her capabilities."

Oh, yeah, she could just imagine what Lindsey's *capabilities* were. Still shivering from Nikos's brief touch, bereft of her baby, Anna could feel her self-control slipping away. She was tired, so tired. She hadn't slept on the plane. She hadn't slept in months.

The truth was, she hadn't really slept since the day Nikos had rejected her in the last trimester of her pregnancy, leaving her to sleep alone every night since.

She rubbed her eyes.

"All right. I think she's vicious and shallow. She's the last person I'd entrust with Misha. Just because she's in your bed it doesn't make her a good caretaker for our son."

He raised a dark eyebrow. "Doesn't it? And yet that's the whole reason that *you* are the caretaker of my son now…because you were once in my bed."

Their eyes met, held. And that was all it took. Memories suddenly pounded through her blood and caused her body to heat five degrees. A hot flush spread across her skin as a single drop of sweat trickled between her breasts. It was as if he'd leaned across the four feet between them and touched her. As if he'd taken possession of her mouth, stroked her bare skin, and pressed his body hot and tight on hers against the wall.

One look from him and she could barely breathe.

He looked away, and she found herself able to breathe again. "And, as usual, you are jumping to the wrong conclusions," he said. "Lindsey is my secretary, nothing more."

Anna had been his secretary once, too. "Yeah, right."

"And whatever her failings," he said, looking at her with hard eyes, "at least she's loyal. Unlike you."

"I never—"

"Never what? Never tricked a bodyguard into taking you to the doctor's office so you could sneak out the back? Never promised to name my son Andreas, then called him something else out of spite? I did everything I could to keep you safe, Anna. You never had to work or worry ever again. All I asked was your loyalty. To me. To our coming child. Was that too much to ask?"

His dark eyes burned through her like acid. She could feel the power of him, see it in the tension of hard muscles beneath his finely cut white shirt.

A flush burned her cheeks. The day of her delivery, surrounded by strangers in a gray Minneapolis hospital, she'd thought of her own great-grandfather, Mikhail Ivanovich Rostov, who'd been born a prince but had fled

Russia as a child, starting a difficult new life in a new land. It had seemed appropriate.

But, whatever her motives, Nikos was right. She'd broken her promise. She pressed her lips together. "I'm…sorry."

She could feel his restraint, the way he held himself in check. "You're sorry?"

"A-about the name."

He was moving toward her now, like a lion stalking a doomed gazelle. "Just the name?"

She backed away, stammering, "But some might say y-you lost all rights to name him when you—" Her heels hit a wall. Nowhere to run. "When you—"

"When I what?" he demanded, his body an inch from hers.

When he'd ruined her father.

When he'd taken a mistress.

When he'd broken her heart…

"Did you ever love me?" she whispered. "Did you love me at all?"

He grabbed her wrists, causing her to gasp. But it was the intensity in his obsidian gaze that pinned her to the wall.

"You ask me that now?" he ground out. But there was a noise down the hall, and he turned his head.

Three maids stood with their arms full of linens, gawking at the sight of their employer pressing Anna against the wall. It probably looked as if they were having hot sex. Heaven knew, they'd done it before, though they'd never been caught.

He lifted a dark eyebrow, and the maids scattered.

With a growl, he grasped Anna's wrist and pulled her into the privacy of the nearby library. He shut the heavy oak door behind him. The sound echoed against the high walls of leatherbound books, bouncing up to the frescoed ceiling, reverberating her doom.

His dark eyes were alight with a strange fire. "You really want to know if I loved you?"

She shook her head, frightened at what she'd unleashed, wishing with all her heart that she could take back the question. "It doesn't matter."

"But it does. To you."

"Forget I asked." She tried desperately to think of a change of subject—anything that would distract him, anything to show that she didn't care. But he was relentless.

"No, I never loved you, Anna. Never. How could I? I told you from the start I'm not a one-woman kind of man. Even if you'd been worthy of that commitment—which obviously you're not."

Pain went through her, but she raised her chin and fired back, "I was loyal to you when no other woman would have been. You kept me prisoner. You fired me from the job I loved. When you took Lindsey in my place I should have left you. But it wasn't until I saw what you did to my father…"

"Ah, yes, your sainted father." He gave a harsh laugh. "Those papers you found, Anna, what did they prove? That I withdrew all financial support from your father's company?"

"Yes. Just when he needed you most. He'd been doing so well, finally getting the company back on its feet, but just when he needed extra cash to open a new factory in China, to compete in the global market—"

"I withdrew my support because I found out that your father embezzled my investment—millions of dollars. There was no new factory, Anna. He'd laid off most of his workers in New York, leaving Rostoff Textiles nothing more than a shell. He used my investment to buy cars and houses and to pay off his gambling debts to Victor Sinistyn."

"No." A knife-stab went through her heart. "It can't be true." But even as she spoke the words she remembered her father's frenetic spending in those days. He'd stopped pressuring her to marry Victor, and instead had suddenly been prosperous, buying a Ferrari for himself, diamonds for Mother, and that crumbling old palace in Russia. He wanted to remind the world of their royalty, he'd said, that the Rostoffs were still better than anyone.

"I didn't tell you," Nikos continued, "or press charges, because I was trying to protect you. I cut off his lines of credit and informed the banks that I was no longer responsible. If he'd just asked me for the money I would have given it to him, for your sake. But he stole from me. I couldn't allow that to continue."

She turned to stare blindly at a nearby gold and lacquer globe. Turning the smooth surface of the world, her fingers rested near St. Petersburg. She wished with all her heart that she was still there, in the dark, cold, crumbling palace without a ruble to her name. She wished Nikos had never found her and dragged her back to luxury. Russia was numb peace compared to this hell.

"And so he went bankrupt. Then died from the shame of it." She closed her eyes, fighting back tears.

"He was weak. And a coward to leave his family behind." She felt his hand on her shoulder as he brushed back her hair with his thick fingers. "I'm done protecting you from the truth. You stole from me. Just like him."

Barely controlling her body's involuntary tremble at his touch, she blinked fast, struggling to contain tears that threatened to spill over her lashes. She pressed her nails hard against her palms. *If he sees me cry, I'll kill myself.*

"I hate you," she whispered.

His grip on her shoulder tightened. "Good. We're even."

"Let me go."

Pressing her back against the wall of leatherbound books, he ran his hand along the bare flesh of her arm. "You chose to come back with me. Did you think it would cost you nothing?"

Heaven help her, but even now, hating him, she wanted to run her hands along his back, to touch the strength of his muscles and the warmth of his skin. She wanted to lace her fingers through the curls of his short dark hair and pull him down to her, to taste the sweet hardness of his mouth.

Oh, God, what had come over her? Trembling from the effort, she forced her body to stay still and betray nothing. "You're not some medieval warlord. You can't toss me in a dungeon and torture me into surrender."

He gently traced the back of his hand down her cheek.

"We have no dungeons here. But I could keep you in my bedroom. Every night. And you wouldn't escape." He whispered in her ear. "You wouldn't want to."

She sucked in her breath as a hard shiver rocked her body. She couldn't stop it even though she knew, pressed against her as he was, he'd be able to feel the movement.

He rewarded her with a smug, masculine smile. "Would you like that, Anna?" he murmured against the soft flesh of her ear, his breath hot on the tender skin of her neck. "Would you like to sleep against me again? Or would I have to tie you to the bed and force you to remember how good it once was between us?"

She felt his closeness and power over her and she hated it, even as part of her longed for him with all the strength of her body's memory.

"I don't want you," she gasped, but even as she spoke the words she felt her traitorous body slide against him, melding every soft curve against his well-muscled form.

"We'll see."

He leaned forward, lowering his head. Involuntarily she closed her eyes, licking her lips as her body moved against him.

She felt the warmth of his breath. She could smell his skin, a scent of soap and hot desert sun and something more—something she couldn't describe but that made her yearn for him with all the ferocity of her heart, as she'd once hungered for Christmas as a child.

But Nikos was in no hurry. The seconds it took before his lips finally touched hers were exquisite torture. And when he finally kissed her the world seemed to whirl around them, making her dizzy, making her knees weak.

She'd expected him to savage her lips, to try and break her in his embrace. But his kiss was gentle. Pure. Just like the very first time he'd kissed her, long ago, that night he'd shown up at her door half-mad with confusion and grief…

He deepened the kiss, brushing his hand through her hair as his tongue caressed her own. She clung to him, returning his caress with a rising passion.

He lingered possessively in her arms, kissing her neck and murmuring endearments in Greek. A sigh of pleasure came from deep within her as she ran her hands through his dark, wavy hair.

Then, without warning, he released her.

She blinked up at him, dazed. Caressing the inside of her wrist with a languorous finger, he looked down at her with cold, dark eyes.

"You hate me enough to kidnap my son," he observed coolly. "But then you kiss me like that."

He dropped her wrist and stepped away from her. As if she disgusted him. Rejecting her. Again.

Her whole body went white-hot with humiliation as she realized that his gentle kiss had been more savage than any forceful assault. Nikos was too strong for brute force. All he had to do was give her the chance to betray herself. One loving, lying kiss from him, and all her feeble defenses had burned to the ground.

She took a deep breath, trying to regain her balance. "You surprised me, that's all. It was just a kiss. It meant nothing."

"It meant nothing to me. But to you…" He looked down at her with a sardonic light in his dark eyes. "I own you, Anna. You're mine in every way. It's time you understood that."

She tightened her hands into fists, fighting for calmness, for some vestige of dignity. "You don't own me. You can't *own* someone."

He stepped back from her. His face was a dark silhouette against the sunlight flooding the high library windows. She could see the cruel twist to his sensual lips as he stared her down.

"You're mine. And I will make you suffer for betraying me."

He meant it, too. She could see that. And she knew how he'd make her suffer. Not by hurting her body— no. But by breaking her will. By breaking her heart. By making her desire him, by giving her pleasure in bed such as she'd never imagined until it ultimately destroyed her soul.

He would poison her with love.

A sob rose to her lips that she couldn't control.

"Enjoy your time with our son," he said. He stepped back through the tall library doors, closing them behind him as he departed with a low, grim parting shot. "Because for the rest of your days and nights you are mine."

Revenge.

As Nikos strode down the hall toward the east wing of the house he smiled grimly, remembering the way Anna had melted into his arms. The bewildered look in her eyes after he pulled away. She was putty in his hands. Like the old song promised, that single kiss had told him everything he needed to know.

She still wanted him.

She still cared for him.

That was her weakness.

Now that he knew, making her suffer would be easier than he'd ever imagined. He'd already begun, by telling her the truth about her worthless excuse for a father. She didn't want his protection? Fine. He was done protecting her.

He would see her twist and pant helplessly, like a butterfly pinned to a display. He would see the pain in her eyes every day while he mercilessly pounded her heart into dust. Maybe then, someday, she would understand what she'd done to him by stealing his child.

His son was all that mattered now. He was the one who needed Nikos's protection…and love.

"I waited for you in the nursery," he heard Lindsey say from down the hall. "When you didn't come, I gave him to the nanny."

He turned to see Lindsey leaning against the wall in a sultry pose. "I was delayed," he replied in a clipped voice.

"That's okay." She skimmed a hand over a tanned thigh barely covered by her short skirt, curving her red lips into a smile. "Finding you alone is even better."

God, no. Another of Lindsey's clumsy attempts at seduction? He was in no mood.

"I gave you the rest of the morning off," he said shortly. "The negotiations for the Singapore bid can wait."

"That's not why I came looking for you."

No, of course it wasn't. Unlike Anna, who'd taken her job so personally, Lindsey would never stick around on a holiday. Her work was barely up to par on regular days.

He hated that he still had Lindsey as his secretary. She wasn't a fraction of the employee Anna had been. He should have fired her long ago. But firing her would have been like admitting that he'd made a mistake.

"What do you want, Lindsey?" he asked wearily.

She toyed with the slit of her short skirt with her long French-manicured nails, making sure he could see the top edge of her thigh-high stockings. "The question is, what do *you* want, Nikos?"

It was the most blatant invitation she'd ever tried.

Once, he might have taken her up on her offer, buried his pain in the sweet oblivion of pleasure. No longer. His experience with Anna had taught him that sex could give a worse hangover than tequila and Scotch.

"Just go to the casino office and wait for my call," he said, walking past her.

Nikos found his son in the nursery, held in the plump arms of his new nanny. The white-haired Scotswoman had recently finished raising an earl's son from babyhood to university, and Nikos had hired her at an exorbitant rate. His son must have the best of everything. "Good morning, Mrs. Burbridge."

"Good morning, sir." She smiled at him, holding up the baby. "Here to hold your son?"

"Of course." But, looking at the baby, he suddenly felt as if he were facing a firing squad. What did he know about babies? He'd never held one before. Nikos had been an only child, or close enough, and he'd never exactly been the sort of man to ooh and ah over the children of friends.

Feeling nervous, Nikos gathered his child from the nanny's protective embrace and held him awkwardly underneath the arms.

"No, er…Mr. Stavrakis, tuck him closer to you. Under his bum."

Nikos tried, but he couldn't seem to get it right. The baby apparently agreed. He looked up at Nikos, and his lower lip started to tremble. He screwed up his face and started to wail.

"I…I seem to be doing this wrong," Nikos said, breaking into a cold sweat.

"Don't take it personally, sir," Mrs. Burbridge said in her friendly Scottish burr. "The bairn is just tired and hungry. He'll soon be right again with a bit to eat. Is his mum about? Or should I make a bottle?"

But Nikos could hardly hear her words over his son's panicked cries. He felt helpless. Useless. *A bad father.*

"He… I… I'll come back when he's not so tired." He thrust the baby back into Mrs. Burbridge's arms and fled.

Or at least he started to. Until he saw Anna standing in the doorway of the nursery, staring around the room with an expression of wonder.

"You didn't change the room," she breathed in amazement. With apparent ease, she took the baby from Mrs. Burbridge and cuddled him close. His cries subsided to small whimpers as Anna looked from the painting of animals and trees on the wall to the soft blue cushions of the window seat. "I was sure you'd have Lindsey redecorate."

Lindsey? Redecorate his house? She could barely manage to type his letters.

"Why would I do that?" Nikos said uncomfortably. "Damn waste of time."

But the truth was he'd loved this nursery. Once. Mostly he'd loved the way Anna's face had lit up when she designed it.

This was the first time he'd been in here since that awful day Cooper had called him to say that Anna was missing. Nikos had been sure she'd been kidnapped. Or worse.

It had been one of the police detectives who'd first dared to ask, "Is it possible the woman's just left you, sir?" Nikos had nearly punched the man for even suggesting it. Because, in spite of his arguments with Anna over her job and her family, Nikos had known he could trust her. He'd never trusted anyone more in his life.

And she'd made him look like a fool.

"Ah, so you're Mum, then? I'm Mrs. Burbridge, the new nanny. A pleasure to meet you, Mrs. Stavrakis."

"I'm not Mrs. Stav— A nanny?" Anna glanced at Nikos in surprise. "Is that really necessary? I can take care of Misha, as I always have."

Nikos stared at the baby. That name still grated on him. He could probably still change it to Andreas. *No*, he thought. Even he thought of his son as Michael now—Misha. Too late to change his name. Too late for a lot of things.

His own son didn't know him. He clenched his hands.

"I'm terribly sorry, Mrs. Burbridge, but we don't need you—"

"Mrs. Burbridge stays," he interrupted, glaring at Anna. "Since I don't know how long you'll be here."

"What do you mean, how long I'll be here?" she demanded. "I'm here until Misha is grown and gone. Unless," she added, "you want to give me joint custody?"

The idea was enough to make him shudder with the injustice of it, but he showed his teeth in a smile. "Your presence here is based upon my will and my son's needs. The day he doesn't need you anymore you'll be escorted to the gate. When he's weaned, perhaps? A few months from now?"

He had the satisfaction of seeing Anna's face go white.

She wasn't the only one. Mrs. Burbridge was edging uncomfortably toward the door. "I…er…now that you're both here with your son, I can see you have much to discuss. I'll go and take my tea, if you'll pardon me…"

Nikos barely noticed the woman leave.

"You can't throw me out," Anna said. "I'm his mother. I have rights."

"You're lucky you're not in jail. You have no idea how much I'd love to hand you to my lawyers. Letting them stomp you like grapes in a vat would give me a great deal of joy."

She looked scared, even as she raised her chin defiantly. "So why don't you do it, then?"

"Because my son needs you. For now." He came closer to her. "But that won't last forever. In the meantime, just give me an excuse, the slightest provocation, and you're out the door."

"You can't force me away from my son!"

"I can't?" He gave her a hard look, then shook his head with a disbelieving snort. "You and your whole aristocratic family really think the world revolves around you and your wants, don't you? To hell with everybody else."

"That's not true!"

"You're too much of a bad influence to raise my child. You're a thief, and the daughter of a thief. Your family mooched off others their whole pathetic lives. Your father was a selfish, immature bastard who never cared about anyone but himself, no matter what it cost the people who loved him—"

He stopped himself, realizing it was no longer Anna's father he was talking about.

She gave him a knowing glance, causing his teeth to set on edge. She knew too damn much. Ever since the night they'd conceived Michael, when he'd been stupid enough to spill his guts, she'd known the chinks in his armor. He hated her for that.

It had been the confusion and pain of finding out about his father that had sent Nikos to her house last year, expecting his perfect secretary to fix the ache as she fixed everything else in his life. But he hadn't expected to end up in Anna's bed. No matter how gorgeous she was, he never would have slept with her if he'd been in his right mind. Anna had been too important to his work—too important in his life—for him to screw it up that way. But, seeking comfort, he'd fallen into her bed and they'd conceived Michael. He'd never had a moment's peace since.

His son started to whimper again.

Anna snuggled the baby close. "You're hungry, aren't you?" With some hesitation, she looked up, biting her lip. "Nikos, I need to feed the baby. Do you mind?"

Itching for a fight, Nikos sat down on the blue overstuffed sofa, pretending to make himself comfortable. "No, I don't mind at all." He indicated the nearby rocking chair.

She stared at him in amazement. "You think I'll do it in front of you?"

"Why not?"

"You're out of your mind."

"What? Are you scared?" He raised his eyebrows. "You have no reason to be. I've seen everything you have to offer."

Although that was true, it wasn't true at all. With her loose ponytail, that left dark tendrils cascading against her white skin, she looked very different from the tightly controlled, buttoned-up woman he remembered. And even in the baggy T-shirt she was wearing he could see that her breasts were larger. They'd been perfect before. He remembered them well, remembered cupping them in his hands, licking slowly across the full nipples, until she'd moaned and writhed beneath him, making love to them after he'd brought her to climax—

twice—with his mouth. What were her breasts like now beneath that shirt?

He suddenly realized he was rock-hard.

He was supposed to torture *her*, not the other way around. He willed the desire away. He didn't want her. He didn't want her.

"Fine. Stay. I don't care," she said, although he could tell by the defiant expression on her beautiful pale face that she cared very much. Grabbing the diaper bag with her free hand, she set it down with a plop on the floor by the cushioned rocking chair. Rummaging through the bag, she pulled out several items before she found a blanket. A small vial fell out and rolled across the floor. He picked it up. The label was in Russian.

"What's this?"

"Baby painkiller," she said. "He's teething."

"At his age?"

"It's a little early, but not uncommon." Her fingers seemed clumsy as she used the blue blanket, decorated with safari animals, to cover both baby and breast before she pulled up her T-shirt. The baby's wails immediately faded to a blissful silence, punctuated with contented gulps.

It shouldn't have been erotic, but it was. Every movement she made, every breath she took, seemed electric in Nikos's overcharged state.

He pressed his lips together, remembering how her whole body had trembled when he'd kissed her in the library. The way she'd melted into his arms when he'd brushed his lips against hers.

And before. After they'd found out she was pregnant he'd barely left her side for six months. Every inch of his skin, every cell of his body tingled with the memory. Remembering lovemaking so hot that it had nearly set his bed on fire. Not just his bed. When they hadn't been fighting about the way he'd forced her to relax and take care of herself, they'd made love everywhere—in the kitchen, the conference room, the home theater. Against the wall in the courtyard one rainy day. And in the back of his helicopter the time he'd wanted to fly her over the Grand Canyon. They'd never made it off the ground.

She glanced up at him now, her turquoise eyes so cool and distant. *I'm too good for you,* her eyes seemed to say. She had a royal bloodline of a thousand years. The great-granddaughter of a Russian princess, she was a fantasy of ice and fire. He'd never experienced any woman like her.

Watching her now, nursing his son, he came to a sudden decision.

She deserved to suffer.

But there was no reason to make himself suffer as well.

Tonight. He would have her in his bed tonight.

CHAPTER THREE

A SLOW burn spread across Anna's cheeks as Nikos watched her nurse their child. She pulled the blanket a little higher, making sure her breast was covered, but she could still feel his eyes on her. It made her feel naked.

Funny to think she'd once dreamed of this moment, of nursing their baby in the gorgeous, spare-no-expense baby suite she'd decorated, with Nikos sitting beside her. A happy family. She'd dreamed that Nikos would love her, be faithful to her, and someday propose to her.

Now the dream tasted like ashes in her mouth.

Perhaps he hadn't purposefully set out to ruin her father, but he'd kept his involvement in his business a secret. If Anna had known, she could have found a way to save her father from himself, to prevent the depression after his bankruptcy that had caused him to drink himself to death. Nikos should have told her. Instead, he'd tried to shield her from everything, as if she were a helpless doll. It was as if the moment she'd become pregnant he'd suddenly lost all trust in her and in the world around them.

Thank God she'd given up on waiting for him to love her. Too bad it had taken her so long to wise up. After five years as his secretary, watching his revolving door policy with women, she'd been stupid to ever think he would ever change.

But for her to run away had been trading one stupidity for another. She'd dragged her newborn baby from Las Vegas to Spain to Paris, always on the run, living in cheap, tiny apartments with paper-thin walls and mattresses that sagged in the middle. Even in her great-grandmother's old palace there'd been no heat or electricity.

That was no life for a baby. In trying to do better for her child, she'd done worse. Nikos had been right to criticize her. Misha deserved a life of comfort and security.

And he deserved to spend time with the father who loved him.

But how could Anna remain here with him and survive? Nikos had made his intentions clear. He would shred her apart without remorse. Glancing at him now, she shivered at the darkness in his eyes. No, she couldn't stay here. That path led to endless days of seduction...a lifetime of heartbreak.

She silently cursed herself. Last year, when Nikos had unexpectedly shown up on her doorstep, she'd opened her arms...her bed...her soul. She should have slammed the door in his face, thrown all her bags into her car and headed east on Interstate 15. If she had, she might have still been in New York. Working. Single. Free.

But then Misha would never have been born.

That focused her. The past didn't matter. Her mistakes were old news. Her son was all that mattered now. And she wasn't going to let him grow up in this cold house with that cold brute.

But how could someone as small and powerless as Anna fight a billionaire ensconced in his own private fortress? He had money, power, and the added immunity of having no heart. What weapons did she have against him? Her family had no money. Her heart was an easy target.

What power did an impoverished single mother have in the world?

Then she had an idea.

An awful, terrible, dangerous idea.

Nikos touched her knee. She jumped in her seat, causing the baby to give a whimper of protest.

"We need to talk. Alone. We'll have Mrs. Burbridge watch Michael tonight." He gave her a lazy smile that belied the predatory look in his eyes. His strong, wide fingers lightly traced the edge of her knee through her jeans. "We'll have dinner. Discuss our future."

Anna could imagine the type of reacquaintance he had in mind. She felt relatively sure that it wouldn't involve a night of bowling or picquet. She trembled with anticipation and fear. He meant nothing less than full-scale seduction—which she wouldn't be able to resist. Even knowing that he caressed her with a cold heart and punishment on his lips.

She cleared her throat. "I would love to have dinner with you tonight, but, um, I'm afraid I have other plans."

He quirked an eyebrow. "Plans?"

"Yes, plans. Big plans." She swayed furiously back and forth in the plush rocking chair.

"Fascinating. With whom?"

She glanced down at the baby. "With a man."

He followed her gaze with amusement. "Anyone I know?"

She scowled, knowing it was hopeless to continue when they both knew that she was a terrible liar. "All right, I'm going to spend the evening with my son."

"Michael won't mind if his parents spend time alone together tonight. Mrs. Burbridge is trustworthy, Anna. She comes highly recommended and I had her thoroughly vetted, believe me. Michael will be happy with her."

"You called him Michael," she said suddenly.

"So? It's his name."

"You accept that?"

She saw a flash of anger in his face which was quickly veiled. "It is done and over with."

"You know I'm sorry about—"

"Forget about it. I have. Let's talk about tonight. Shall we have Cavaleri serve us dinner under the stars? By the pool?"

Yeah, the pool. Which was conveniently adjacent to the poolhouse, the Moroccan stone fountain, and the manmade waterfall—all places where they'd made love during their brief months of happiness.

Not happiness, she reminded herself fiercely. *Illusion.*

"No thanks," she said. "I heard it might rain tonight."

"Would you prefer we have dinner at L'Hermitage?"

Her breath caught at his suggestion. L'Hermitage Casino Resort. All the years she'd spent organizing the details of its creation, and she hadn't even seen the inside since it opened. She ached to see it. In so many ways L'Hermitage was a part of her. She and Nikos had worked on it together. She'd never formally studied architecture, or interior design, but he'd still taken her suggestions to heart. She missed that.

"We'll have dinner at Matryoshka," Nikos continued.

Yes, her heart yearned. But she forced herself to take the safe course. She turned away.

"You can do whatever you want," she said crisply. "But after Misha's asleep I will stay in my room alone. I plan to get a sandwich and take a long, hot bath."

He gave her another lazy half-smile, toying with her. "That sounds pleasant. I'll join you."

"You'll find a locked door."

"This is my house, Anna. Do you really think you can keep me out?"

She took a deep breath. He was right, of course. He had the key to every lock. And even if he didn't, he could break down the door with one slam of his powerful arms. He'd find a way into her room, and that would be that.

Of course he wouldn't need violence. One kiss and she'd fall at his feet like a harem girl, without a mind or will of her own.

Victor. The name of the Very Bad Idea pounded in her brain. He was her only hope to escape. Her only hope to survive.

It's too dangerous, she tried to argue with herself. But her former employer had ties both in Las Vegas and in Russia, and the wealth to employ lawyers who could face the best Nikos had to offer. The two men already hated each other—ever since the day Nikos had stolen Anna away to be his executive secretary. If Victor was still in love with her, he'd be willing to help… For a price. Whose price was worse?

Talk about a rock and a hard place. Would there be any way for her to pit the two men against each other and emerge unscathed, without giving body and soul to either one?

She glanced at Nikos from beneath her lashes. His power seemed like a tangible thing. It scared her. No, she couldn't risk getting Victor involved. It was too dangerous. Someone would end up getting hurt.

With as much grace as she could muster, she gently lifted Misha out from beneath the blanket, pulling down her shirt.

"He's asleep," she said softly. She carefully laid him down on the soft mattress of the crib. Nikos came to stand beside her, and for a moment they watched their child sleep. The baby's arms were tossed carelessly above his head, and his long dark eyelashes fluttered against his plump, rosy cheeks as his breath rose and fell. She whispered, "Isn't he beautiful?"

"Yes."

She bit her lip at his abrupt tone, feeling guilty again about what she'd done. No matter how she hated him, how could she have separated a child from his father?

She took a deep breath. "I...I owe you an apology, Nikos. I should never have taken Misha away from you."

"No." His voice was low.

She licked her lips. Might as well get it all over with. "And I'm sorry for blaming you for my father's death," she said in a rush. "You invested in his company and he took advantage of you. He's the one who chose to drink himself to death. I just wish you'd told me, so I could have tried to do something to save him before it was too late." She paused, then sighed. "I guess we've both made a mess of things in our own way, haven't we?"

He drew back, his eyes cold. "My only mistake was trying to take care of you."

She was trying to be penitent, but his words caused resentment to surge through her anew. She backed away from the crib, keeping her voice soft so as not to wake their sleeping child. "Oh, I see," she said furiously. "So was it for my *welfare* that you cheated on me during my pregnancy?"

He followed her across the room, clenching his jaw in exasperation. He shook his head. "What are you talking about? I never cheated on you. Although at this point I wish I had. Are you trying to make up lies to use against me in court? That's a new low, even for you."

She could hardly believe he'd try to deny it. "What about Lindsey?"

"What about her?"

"You might as well admit she was your mistress. She told me everything." Anna stared blindly at the five-foot-high stuffed giraffe sitting on the powder-blue sofa in the corner. "Lindsey often came here during the last months of my pregnancy, supposedly to ask questions about her job. But I think the real reason was to torment me with details of your affair."

For a moment there was silence in the shaded cool of the nursery.

"Lindsey told you that we were lovers?" His voice was matter-of-fact, emotionless.

"She told me everything." Her throat started to hurt as the pain went through her heart again, ripping the wound anew. "How often you made love. How she believed you'd ask her to marry you."

"It's a lie."

"Of course *that* part was a lie. She was obviously delusional. You'll never propose to anyone." She gave a bitter laugh. "I almost feel sorry for her. You use women when it suits you. But you'll abandon her like you abandoned me."

He became dangerously still. "You think I—abandoned you?"

"I wasn't so sexy anymore, was I? The last three months of my pregnancy you wouldn't touch me, you pushed me away, and finally you just left altogether. You replaced me with a younger, slimmer model."

He looked down at her with narrowed eyes as his nostrils flared. "And that's really what you really think of me? After all our years working together you think I would reject and abandon the woman carrying my child."

She pushed away all the wonderful memories of

them working, laughing, dancing together. Of nights under the stars. Days spent together in bed.

Wordlessly, she nodded.

"Damn you, it's well known that having sex during the final trimester can induce early labor—"

"I had a healthy pregnancy!" Anna cried. "But you kept me prisoner for nine months. I let you do it because I thought you were just worried about our child. But you kept me away from my family and my work, keeping me helpless and alone. Then you left to live with your gorgeous young mistress. Make up some cockamamie story about early labor if you want, but the truth is you just didn't want me anymore!"

"Anna, you know that's not—"

"I gave you everything, and you broke my heart." She turned away, barely holding back tears as she looked down at her sleeping son. "Go, Nikos. Just leave. That's what you do best, isn't it?"

He grabbed her shoulders, whirling her around. "I can't believe this. *That's* why you kidnapped my son and caused me four months of hell? Because of some damned lies Lindsey told you?"

His hands tightened painfully, and she was suddenly aware of his body close to hers. His breath brushed her cheek, sending waves of heat up and down her body. Her gaze fell to his mouth.

She licked her own lips unconsciously. "Lindsey is your lover. Why won't you just admit it? You didn't hesitate to tell me the brutal truth this morning about my father. I thought you said you were done protecting me!"

He pulled her close, wrapping his muscled arms tightly around her as he whispered in her ear, "Damn you, Anna."

He abruptly released her, striding for the door.

"I'll be back for dinner," he tossed at her without a backward glance. "I expect you to be waiting for me when I return."

She stared after him, still shivering. She had no doubt as to what he expected of her. To be waiting for him in lingerie, holding two flutes of champagne, hot and ready for his seduction. He thought she was weak. He thought that, even though she hated him, she would be powerless to resist.

No, she thought. No way.

Resting one hand protectively on her son's crib, Anna narrowed her eyes.

Whether he was more dangerous or not, Anna had to get Victor's help so she could get out of this house. She had no choice. Because when Nikos had told her that Lindsey's words were lies, she'd found herself wanting to believe him. Aching to believe him.

Being this close to Nikos was killing her.

She'd go to Victor's club tonight. She'd beg for his help. In exchange, she would promise to work for him again—something she'd sworn she'd never do. She'd do anything short of becoming his lover. And once she had Victor's help Nikos would see who was powerless and weak.

She clenched her hands into fists, remembering the arrogant way he'd demanded that she wait for him tonight. She'd be waiting, all right.

Waiting to give him the shock of his life.

* * *

Nikos poured himself a small bourbon from the crystal decanter in his office on the fourth floor of L'Hermitage.

He swished the glass and leaned back against the desk, staring out through the wide windows overlooking the Las Vegas Strip. The brilliant blue sky and desert sun were beating down on the palm trees and garish architecture. The blacktop of Las Vegas Boulevard reflected waves of heat on the camera-wielding tourists, the gamblers and the drunken, ecstatic newlyweds.

He took a sip of bourbon. The normally smooth flavor was tasteless. Staring at the amber-colored liquid, he set down the glass and rested his head against his hands.

At last he understood.

He'd thought Anna had left because he'd tried to protect her during her pregnancy. He'd fired her because he'd sworn he'd be damned if his child's mother would ever have to work—not after he'd watched his own mother work herself to death. He'd blocked Anna's phone calls because he'd too often found her pacing while she solved problems at the casino building site, or tried to solve the endless foolish problems of her mother and sister. In both cases she'd been taking on problems that other people should have handled for themselves. Her first priority should have been her child, to the exclusion of all else. Why had she not seen that? Why had she been unable to let the weight of responsibility rest on him? Why had she fought his efforts to keep his fragile new family safe and protected?

Perhaps he should have told her about her father's

initial request for an investment, but Alexander Rostoff had asked Nikos to keep it quiet. Later, when Nikos had discovered the embezzlement, Anna was already pregnant, and upsetting her had been the last thing he'd wanted to do. Anna already took too much on where her family was concerned.

But he couldn't believe that his real mistake, what had truly driven Anna away, had been leaving her bed.

She'd been so beautiful in her final trimester, lush with curves and ripe with his child, that Nikos had known there was no way he could keep his hands off her. He'd read in a pregnancy book that late-term sex could be a factor in early labor, so he'd forced himself to leave her, moving to his newly finished penthouse at L'Hermitage. To an empty bed and a lonely apartment. For her sake. For their child's sake.

And she'd taken that as rejection?

In leaving Anna's bed he'd given up the greatest pleasure he'd ever known. He'd even told her why he was leaving, but apparently she hadn't believed him. Instead of being grateful, she'd been angry at his sacrifice.

He clenched his jaw. Hell, how could she have felt otherwise after what Lindsey had told her?

Furious, he rose from his desk and paced his office, crossing to the opposite wall of one-sided windows that overlooked the main casino floor. Leaning against the glass, he stared down at the wide expanse of elegant nineteenth-century Russian architecture, the soaring ceilings with high crystal chandeliers and gilded columns, packed in with slot machines, card tables and well-heeled gamblers.

He spotted Lindsey weaving through the crowds, rushing toward the employee elevator. She was carrying a bag from a high-end lingerie store in the Moskva Shopping Complex within the casino. Even after he'd ordered her to wait for him here at the office she'd taken time to go shopping. Unbelievable.

He missed Anna.

Anna, the perfect secretary. Anna, who'd read his mind. Anna, who'd solved problems before he'd even known they existed.

He'd first met her in New York, when Victor Sinistyn had pitched that ridiculous idea for an Elvis-themed hotel-casino called Girls Girls Girls. The meeting had been an utter waste of his time. With twenty boutique hotels around the world, Stavrakis Resorts were known for their elegance, not for their go-go dancers.

Nikos had noticed Sinistyn's executive assistant, with her cool efficiency and aristocratic demeanor. He'd needed someone who could handle the complex details of running a billion-dollar business while still maintaining the image of his company. He'd needed someone with understanding and discretion, who wouldn't let herself be bullied—not even by him.

Anna Rostoff had been everything he'd wanted and more. Hiring her away from Victor Sinistyn had caused him no end of grief, for the man had been a furious thorn in his side ever since. But Sinistyn's enmity had been a small price to pay. For five years he and Anna had worked together, traveling around the world in his private jet, often working around the clock. She'd never complained. She'd never failed him. She'd never made a mistake. And he'd compensated her accordingly. When he'd found out she was sending most of her salary to support her mother and younger sister in New York, he'd given her a raise that had sent her salary skyrocketing deep into six figures.

He'd known by then that she was indispensable to his empire. Indispensable to *him*.

"I'm here." Lindsey's voice was panting as she leaned against the doorway. She'd stashed the lingerie bag somewhere *en route*, and now brought a hand to her heaving chest. "I was...um..."

"Stuck in traffic?" he said laconically.

"Right. Stuck in traffic." She looked relieved. "You know Las Vegas Boulevard is a nightmare this time of day."

"Don't worry." Standing over his desk, he leaned forward and gave her a lazy smile. "You're just in time."

"In time?" Her eyes lit up, and her hips swayed as she came toward him. Harsh afternoon sunlight hit her tanned face as she stretched a manicured hand to caress his cheek. "Past time, I'd say."

He removed Lindsey's hand.

"Stop it, Lindsey. It's not going to happen."

The desire for release was strong in him. The desire to forget, to bury himself in flesh and curves and the hot scent of woman. To pull her long hair back, exposing her throat for plunder, to possess her mouth and see the answering spark of desire in her eyes...

He wanted a woman. God, yes. Just not this one.

He wanted the woman who was at home right now, hating him.

Undeterred, Lindsey stroked his thigh. "Why do you think I took this stupid job? I know we'd be perfect together. I'll make you wild. I'll make you so hot and worked up that you'll forget that tramp—"

He cut her off, his tone ruthlessly cold. "You told Anna that we were lovers. When she was pregnant and vulnerable you lied to her. I want to hear it from your mouth."

"All right." Lindsey dropped the seductive pose, and her young, pretty face took on the hard, calculating look of a hustler. "But, the way I see it, I was doing you a favor."

He turned to his desk and pressed a button. Two guards appeared at his door.

"Please escort Miss Miller out of the casino," he said coldly. "Her employment here is done."

The color drained from her face, leaving her pale beneath her tan. "What?"

"A severance check will be waiting for you at the casino office downstairs. You'll find I've been more generous than you deserve."

"You can't be serious!"

"For every minute you argue with me I'll instruct Margaret to subtract a thousand dollars from your check."

She sucked in her breath. "Fine!" She turned on her designer heel and stalked out, grabbing her shopping bag just outside the door. She stopped and glared at him.

"It's not my fault she left, you know. She was having your kid and you still wouldn't marry her. Pathetic." She shook the lingerie bag at him. "And now you'll never see me in *this*!"

He should have gotten rid of her a long time ago, he mused, his ears still ringing with the noise of the slammed door. It took him a moment to realize he was hearing the phone. Shaking his head, he picked up the receiver.

"Yeah?"

"You're not going to like this, boss," Cooper said.

"What's wrong?" Nikos's heart gave a weird thump. "Michael?"

"The baby's fine. With his nanny. But Anna took off. I didn't stop her, since she didn't take the boy. I had her followed, like you said. She took the Maserati."

Nikos nearly choked on his bourbon. Anna had snuck out? Leaving their son behind? When it was almost dusk? Driving his favorite car?

That was her idea of going under the radar?

"Where did she go?"

"That's the part you're not going to like." Coop paused. "She walked into Victor Sinistyn's club ten minutes ago."

"And you waited ten minutes to tell me?" he said tersely.

"Wait, boss. You don't want to go there alone—I'm getting some of the guys—"

"I can do this alone!"

Nikos slammed down the phone and headed for the door. He went straight to his private garage and jumped on his Ducati motorcycle. Swerving through the traffic on Las Vegas Boulevard, he headed downtown.

Fremont Street was gritty, for all of its brilliant lights. This was where the hardcore gamblers came to play, far from the lavish themed hotels and the families with cameras and strollers. This was the original Las Vegas, and its hard-edged glamor showed its tarnish like an aging showgirl.

Victor Sinistyn had turned his failed casino concept into a dance club. Outside of Girls Girls Girls there was a long line of lithe, scantily-clad twenty-somethings, waiting to drink and dance.

Nikos leapt off his motorcycle, tossing his keys to a valet. The bouncer recognized Nikos as he strode arrogantly forward, bypassing the line.

"No bodyguards tonight, Mr. Stavrakis?"

"Where's your boss?" Not waiting for an answer, Nikos pushed past him.

Inside the club, colored lights were pulsing through the darkness to the beat of the music. The place was a cavern, a rebuilt warehouse with an enormous high ceiling, and it shook with the rhythm of the dancing crowd. The air was steamy, hot, redolent of sex and skin.

And then he saw her, wearing a tiny halter top and low-slung jeans that made her look virtually naked.

Dancing with Victor Sinistyn.

The man smiled down at Anna as they danced, running his hands possessively down her bare skin. She gave him a strained smile as she stepped back from him, swaying her body, moving down to her knees before she rose again. She leaned back, arms over her head, and her full breasts strained the fabric, nearly popped out of her flesh-colored top. But apparently Sinistyn wasn't satisfied with just looking.

Grabbing her shoulders, he pulled her bare belly against him and ground his body against hers, nuzzling her neck. Anna didn't struggle, but Nikos had a glimpse of her pale face. She looked as if she were gasping for air. Why was Anna allowing him to manhandle her?

He saw the Russian's hands move toward her breasts. With a savage growl, Nikos started to push roughly through the crowd. All he could think was that if Sinistyn kept touching her he'd kill the man in his own club.

CHAPTER FOUR

"There, we've had our dance." Anna panted, drawing away. "Please can we talk now?"

"The music's not over yet," Victor said, pulling her back close.

That was what she was afraid of—that this music would never end. Her skin crawled where he'd touched her. "But I need to ask you something important, Victor. A life-and-death favor."

"Then you should be trying to please me now," Victor replied, flashing his teeth in a grin as he moved his body against hers. He was handsome, Anna thought, amid the heat and the lights and the pounding rhythm of the dance music. She could see why her sister had had a crush on him since girlhood. Too bad he had such an ugly soul.

Aware that she was playing with fire, Anna wanted to run from him, far away from this dance floor.

But where would she go?

Besides, though he might have hurt business rivals in the past, he would never hurt her, she tried to reassure herself. She'd known Victor since she was eighteen years old, when he'd gone into business with her father and had personally asked Anna to become his secretary. True, she'd spent five years fending him off, but now she had no other choice but to ask for his help. If she didn't want to be completely at Nikos's mercy she needed a favor from the only man who could fight him and win.

"Victor—"

"Call me Vitya, like you used to."

That was Natalie's nickname for him, not hers. "Victor, please, if we could only—"

A hand suddenly gripped her wrist, pulling her away.

"Get away from her, Sinistyn," Nikos said.

"Stavrakis." Narrowing his eyes, Victor wrapped his arm around Anna's waist, pulling her back so hard he almost yanked her off her feet. "You've got some nerve to come into my club and start throwing orders. Get out before I throw you out."

"You? You'll throw me out? Or do you mean one of your goons will do it for you?" Nikos drawled lazily, in a tone that belied the threat in his posture. "We both know you wouldn't have the guts to do it yourself."

Victor smiled at him, showing sharp teeth. He looked over the dance floor. Anna noticed his bodyguards hovering close by. Apparently, this gave Victor courage. "I don't see Cooper with you tonight. It was a mistake to leave your guard dogs at home, you Greek—"

Anna physically came between them, pushing them apart. She felt sick. She'd thought Nikos would wait for his bodyguards, giving her at least thirty minutes to privately conclude her business with Victor. Having him come so quickly, and alone, had shot her plan apart.

"Please, let me go," she said to Victor. "I need to talk to Nikos anyway. I—I'll talk to you more later."

For a moment Victor looked as if he were going to pummel the smirk off Nikos's face anyway. Then he shrugged and said shortly, "As you wish, *loobemaya*. Go. Until later."

He walked off the dance floor. Nikos looked as if he meant to deliver some rejoinder, but Anna grabbed his hands, forced his attention back to her. "What are you doing here?"

Nikos's anger came back to focus on her. "The question, madam, is what are *you* doing here? Dancing with him? Dressed like that?"

"I can dress as I please—"

He interrupted her. "You will never see Victor Sinistyn again, do you understand?"

"No, I don't. You're not my husband. You're nothing—"

With a growl, he dragged her off the floor, through the crowds and out of the club. She struggled, unable to escape his iron grip.

Outside, the cooling desert air felt fresh against her overheated skin. She took several deep breaths, trying to calm her fears as he retrieved his motorcycle from the valet.

This was going to work. It *had* to work. She'd use the threat of Victor to force Nikos to give her joint custody of her son. And set her free.

Tossing a tip to the valet, Nikos threw a muscular leg over the motorcycle's seat. For a moment Anna's gaze lingered on his body, on the way his snug black T-shirt accentuated the muscles of his chest and his flat belly, on the tight curve of his backside in the dark designer jeans.

"Get on," he ordered, his eyes like ice.

Carefully, Anna climbed up behind him on the motorcycle. She gave a little squeak as he revved the engine and roared down the street without a word of warning.

She held him close, her body pressed against his back. Her tight suede halter top thrust her breasts upward, and they felt exquisitely sensitive, the nipples hardening as they brushed against the muscles of his back. She tightened her grip on his waist, her dark hair flying in the wind.

"You'll never go to that club again," he said in a low voice, barely audible over the roar of the engine.

"I'll do as I please."

"Promise me right now, or I swear to God I'll turn around and burn the place to the ground."

She felt his body tense beneath her grip as he waited. His deliciously hard body felt so good beneath her hands. It was enough to make her lose all rational thought.

Perhaps she could give in to this one request, she thought. She didn't want to go back to the stupid club again, anyway. She had no intention of letting Victor paw at her more on the dance floor.

Next time she'd meet him somewhere else. Like a library.

"All right," she said. "I promise."

She felt his body relax slightly. "Good."

A few moments later he pulled the motorcycle beneath the brilliant marquee of L'Hermitage Casino Resort.

Like the Parisian and Venetian hotels down the street, L'Hermitage's architecture was an imposing fantasy. Much of the design had been based upon the stately nineteenth-century palaces of St. Petersburg, but the centerpiece of the building was a reproduction of St. Basil's Cathedral in Red Square, with its distinctive onion-shaped domes.

Tossing his keys to the valet, he took her by the hand—more gently this time—and led her through the front door for her first inside look at the finished project that had consumed them both for nearly four years.

She gazed upward at the high ceiling as he led her through the main floor of the casino. The architecture had triangular shaped Russian arches over doors, watched over by painted angels. Soaring above the slot machines and roulette tables, a simulated horizon held the breathless hush of a starlit sky on a cold winter night.

"It's beautiful," she whispered.

He smiled at her then, an open, boyish smile, and it nearly took her breath away. "Wait until you see the rest."

On the other side of the main casino floor they entered the Moskva Shopping Complex, which was built like several outdoor streets within the casino. The storefronts and streetlights, the ambient light and even the sounds of birds far overhead, made Anna feel as if she was walking through a fairytale Russian city.

"It's just like I dreamed." She looked at the expensive shops, Gucci and Prada and Tiffany, and her fingers tightened around his. "You made our dream a reality."

He stared at her, then slowly shook his head. "We did it together, Anna. I couldn't have created L'Hermitage without you."

She blinked as tears filled her eyes. He appreciated all the work she'd done, the heart she'd poured into her work.

He looked her full in the face. "I've missed you."

Anna felt her heart stop right in the middle of the ebb and flow of the busy street. The chic people hurrying into the stores seemed to blur around her. Could it be true? Just by seeing her with Victor, could Nikos have realized he missed her? Needed her?

Loved her?

Her heart gave a strange thump. Words trembled on her lips. Horrible words she couldn't possibly say, because they couldn't possibly be true. Could they?

"You…you've missed me?"

"Of course," he replied. "No other secretary has ever been your equal."

"Oh." The thump moved from her heart to her throat. She turned to face the large building behind her.

"Matryoshka," she murmured, over the miserable lump in her throat. She stared up at the restaurant's imposing domes of unpainted wood, like a miniature cathedral tucked inside the fairytale street. She had to change the subject before he realized what she'd been thinking. Before she despised herself more for being foolish enough to think he actually cared for her.

"Wait until you see the inside," he said, taking her hand. "You'll think you're inside the Terem Palace."

A slender, well-dressed *maître d'* stood at a podium just inside the restaurant.

"We'd like the table by the window," Nikos said.

The *maître d'* didn't bother looking up from his reservation page. "That particular table is booked for four months," he said, sounding bored. "And we have nothing available for tonight—not a thing—not even if you were the King of—"

Mid-sneer, the man glanced up. He saw Nikos, and his jaw went slack. He suddenly began to cough.

"One moment, sir," he said breathlessly. "We'll get your table ready, for you and for your lovely lady, straight away."

Two minutes later the *maître d'*, now fawning and polite, had left them at the best table in the restaurant. A little awed in spite of herself, Anna looked around.

The interior of Matryoshka had been designed in seventeenth-century Muscovite style, with intimate low ceilings made of stucco and covered with frescoes of interweaving flowers and the nesting dolls that inspired the restaurant's name. Elaborate tiled ovens and *kokoshnik*-shaped arches were lit by flickering candles on the tables and torches on the walls.

As a waiter came to tell them about the specials, Nikos cut him off. "We'll both have the salmon with caviar and champagne sauce," he said, closing his menu. "And Scotch—neat."

"Wait." Anna stopped the waiter with a hand on his

arm. "I would like Chicken Kiev, please. And *kulich* for dessert," she added, referring to the Easter fruitcake. "And sparkling water to drink." She closed her menu, matching Nikos glare for glare. "Not Scotch."

Caught in the crossfire, the waiter glanced nervously at Nikos, who nodded.

After the young man was gone, Nikos bit out, "I didn't mean the Scotch for you. I know you're nursing."

"Even if I weren't nursing I wouldn't want it. Or caviar, either. Ugh."

He gave her a humorless smile. "A Russian who dislikes caviar? Next you'll be telling me you have no taste for vodka."

"I don't appreciate you trying to order for me. I'm not a child."

"I was treating you like a lady," he said coolly, leaning back in his chair.

"Oh? And is that how you justify telling me who my friends can be?"

"Sinistyn's not your friend," Nikos bit out. "He'll use you and toss you aside."

She gave him an angry glare. "And you want to be the only one who does that to me?"

As the waiter placed their drinks on the table, Nikos looked affronted, furious. "You cannot even compare—"

"Save it. I've known Victor since I was eighteen. Our fathers were friends—although they chose to make their living in very different ways. I was Victor's secretary for five years. I know him better than you do."

Unfortunately she understood him well enough to

know that everything Nikos said about him was true. But she wasn't going to say that.

Nikos's hands clenched on the table. "Just how *well* do you know him?"

Anna tilted her head and watched him narrowly. "He's asked me to marry him several times."

He glanced at the stained-glass window. The expression on his face was half hidden, but his jaw was hard. "What?"

"I've always said no, but that might change. I won't be your pawn, Nikos. I won't take your punishment forever. I won't allow you to threaten me with losing my child. And if what it takes to match you is to marry Victor…"

She let her voice trail off.

Nikos blinked, very slowly. When he opened his eyes, for the first time since he'd dragged her back to Las Vegas, they were wary. He was looking at her not as a victim to punish but as a challenging adversary. "What do you want?"

"You know what I want. My freedom."

"I won't let you take Michael from me. Ever. Get that."

"Then you can expect a very prolonged custody battle. If Victor and I take you to court, it'll be splashed in the papers. A full media circus."

"Is that really what you want?" he said in disbelief. "The two of us pulling at our child like a rope in a tug-of-war?"

"Of course not!" She had no intention of starting a romance with Victor, let alone making him Misha's stepfather, but she was praying Nikos wouldn't call her bluff. "I don't want to ask Victor for help, but what choice have you given me?"

The torches around them flickered in silence for several seconds before Nikos tossed his napkin down on the table. "Fine. You win."

Nikos abruptly rose from the chair. Anna watched in amazement as he strode across the restaurant and out the door.

She'd won?

He was going to give her joint custody? He was going to let her leave Las Vegas? Let her have her own life back?

She could hardly believe it. In a few days she'd be back in New York, looking for a new job. She knew she wouldn't find anything as invigorating as working at Stavrakis, but at least she'd be able to take pride in supporting herself and her son. Nikos would insist on child support, of course, but she'd put that money into a trust fund for Misha later. That way it would be clear to everyone, including herself, that Nikos had no hold on her. She'd never give him power over her again.

And to make sure of that she wanted some space between them. The whole country would be a nice start.

Their dinners were served, and she took a bite of her Chicken Kiev. Delicious. She stared into the flickering flame of the torch on the wall. It had almost been too easy. She was actually disappointed Nikos had capitulated so quickly. After the way he'd treated her, her blood had been up for a fight.

"Enjoying your meal?" the waiter asked, refilling her water glass with a smile. "You look happy."

"I am."

"Because you're in love? I am too," the young man added, and before she could dispute his assumption he leaned forward to joyfully whisper, "I'm proposing to my girlfriend tonight."

"That's wonderful!"

"But what's this?" He peered at Nikos's untouched plate. "Mr. Stavrakis didn't like his salmon?"

"He, um, got called away." Anna handed the waiter her own empty plate, which she'd all but licked clean. If it weren't for the caviar spread over the salmon, she'd have eaten Nikos's dinner, too.

"In that case, I'll bring your dessert. An extra big slice," he promised, then winked at her. "Everyone should celebrate tonight."

She definitely felt like celebrating. But as she dug into the fruitcake a few moments later she noticed her breasts were starting to hurt. Back at the estate, Misha would be getting hungry. She needed to return to the dance club, retrieve the Maserati and get back.

"Is there anything else I can do for you, miss?" the waiter asked.

"Um…the bill?"

"Mr. Stavrakis always takes care of his guests. I'd lose my job if I brought you a bill. Sorry. Standing orders."

She breathed a sigh of relief. Matryoshka was very expensive. As it had been Nikos's choice to bring her here, and he'd ditched her in the middle of the meal, her conscience would allow him to pay. Heck, his accountants would probably get a tax advantage out of it.

But just as she was about to leave Nikos sat down heavily in the chair across from her.

"What are you doing here?" she blurted out, chagrined. Could he have already gotten a lawyer to draw up the custody papers?

He frowned at the empty table. "Where is my dinner?"

"Long gone. My Chicken Kiev was delicious, though." She shook her head wryly. "Thanks for ditching me. I had a nice conversation with the waiter. He's in love. He's going to propose," she said airily.

"To you?" Nikos said sharply.

Anna snorted a derisive laugh. "Yes. To me. I have that kind of power over men."

He took a small sip of Scotch. Casually, almost dismissively, he tossed a small box on the table, pale blue as a robin's egg. "Here."

Frowning, she opened it.

Inside the box, nestled on black velvet, she saw a huge diamond ring set in platinum. The facets of the enormous stone, which had to be at least ten carats, sparkled up at her in the candlelight. It took her breath away.

She twisted her great-grandmother's stoneless ring around her finger nervously. Nikos's diamond was so big it wouldn't have even fit inside the Princess's empty setting. The diamond was bigger than a marble. Excessive to the point of tackiness. And yet…

She swallowed, looking up at him. "What is this? Some kind of trick?"

"No trick," he said. "We will be married tonight."

The rush that went through her then was like nothing

she'd ever felt. *Nikos wanted to marry her.* Just as she'd dreamed for so long. Even when she'd known it was impossible—even when, as his secretary, she'd watched him go from one sexual conquest to another, she'd had secret dreams that she might someday be the woman to tame him.

"Put it on," Nikos said.

But it wasn't the earnest pleading of a lover—it was an order. Utterly cold and without emotion.

And just like that the pleasure in her heart evaporated.

Nikos didn't want to marry her.

He wanted to *own* her.

This was his way of dealing with the threat of Victor. Rather than calling for his lawyer, rather than negotiating for joint custody of Misha, he figured it was easier to just buy her off with a ring. He thought Anna could be purchased for the price of a two-hundred-thousand dollar trinket and some meaningless words.

"What do you take me for?" she said in a low voice.

"As my wife. To have—" his eyes raked over her "—and to hold."

She swallowed. His dark eyes were undressing her, right there in the restaurant. As if he were considering the very real possibility of pulling her to him, ripping off her clothes, and making love to her on there on the table, with the entire restaurant watching.

He still intended to coldly seduce her. He still meant to take his pound of flesh for what she'd done. And if he were her husband, his power over her would increase tenfold.

Just give in, her thought whispered. Give in to her

desire. Give in to his power. Then he couldn't send her away from Misha ever again. She would be his wife. She would be above Lindsey and the other women like her— she would be Mrs. Stavrakis. And though Nikos hated her now, perhaps someday…

No. She had to get a hold of herself. Even if someday Nikos forgave her, she would never, ever forgive him. He didn't love her. And it was worse than that. He didn't even trust her enough to work or to make any decisions about her own life.

He said he wanted to protect her, but he really wanted to lock her away, like a parakeet in a tiny gold cage.

Could she put aside every ounce of pride and self-preservation and marry a man who hated her? Allow herself to be bound to him forever?

"No," she whispered.

His dark eyebrows pushed together like a storm-cloud. "What did you say?"

She trembled at his anger even as she braced herself for more. She wouldn't bend. She wouldn't submit. She wouldn't sell herself for the hopeless, destructive illusion that he might someday trust her, respect her, love her.

"I said no." Snapping the box shut, she held it out to him. "Sorry, Nikos. I'm not for sale."

CHAPTER FIVE

NIKOS stared at her, hardly able to believe his ears.

"Don't you understand?" he said. "I'm giving you what you wanted. I'm making you my wife."

"How very generous. But I only wanted that when I was in love with you. Not anymore." When he didn't take the box, she tossed it on the table between them. Such a small thing, but it separated them like a stone wall two feet thick. "Now I just want to be free."

She shifted in her chair, brushing her dark hair off her bare shoulders. He looked around the restaurant that they'd conceived together. To his fevered imagination it seemed that every man in the room was watching Anna. Her lovely pale skin, the dark hair cascading in riotous waves down her back, those almond-shaped turquoise eyes challenging him. The beige halter top barely covered her full breasts, and her dark low-rise jeans revealed her flat belly.

God, she was gorgeous. He'd never wanted her more.

"You will marry me, Anna," he said. "We both know it will happen."

"Death and taxes are inevitable. But marriage?" She gave him a humorless smile. "No."

"I don't particularly want to marry you, either. But my son's happiness means more to me than my own."

He saw her lips tighten at that. Good, so she understood how much he cared for Michael.

But there was more to it than that.

From the moment Nikos had seen Anna dancing with Victor Sinistyn in the club, something had changed in him that he couldn't explain. He only knew that Anna belonged to him and no other man. He had to stamp his possession on her for all the world to see.

The idea had haunted him. In the club, on his motorcycle, as he'd walked with Anna through the casino. He'd kept thinking it would be simple enough to marry her. Hell, they were already in Las Vegas. And once she wore his ring he knew she would be utterly loyal to those vows. There would be no more arguments or fear of betrayal. No custody battle splashed in the papers. It was the perfect solution.

He'd just never thought she would refuse him.

"You will marry me for the sake of our son."

"Never."

Nikos raked a hand through his dark hair in frustration. This wasn't how it was supposed to go. He was accustomed to his employees rushing to fulfill his orders, and his mistresses had always done the same.

"You will be rich—richer than your wildest dreams," he pointed out. "I will deny you nothing."

She snorted incredulously. "You think I care about that? If I'd wanted to marry for money, I could have done it long ago."

"Meaning you'd have married Victor Sinistyn?"

"Yes. I could have." She paused. "I could still."

Nikos tightened his hands into fists, cracking his knuckles. A flood of unwelcome emotion swept through him.

He remembered watching Anna in the dance club, the way she'd swayed against Sinistyn, gyrating beneath the flashing lights. He remembered the way the skin on her taut belly had glistened, how her low-slung jeans had barely covered her hips as she swayed.

No other man but Nikos should touch her. Ever.

Especially not Victor Sinistyn. How could Nikos allow Anna to throw herself away on a man like that? How could he allow his son to have this man for a stepfather.

There was only one way to make sure that never happened. She would agree to his proposal.

He had to convince her.

"Why don't you give the ring to Lindsey?" Anna said sweetly as she rose from the table. "I'm sure she'd be more than willing to marry you. Now, if you'll excuse me, I need to go home and feed my son."

Home.

He had a sudden image of her in bed, and he relaxed. Bed was a place where they'd always understood one another very well. A slow smile spread across his lips. Once they were home he would take her in his arms and she would not be able to deny him anything…

"I will take you home," he said.

"But I left your car at the club—"

"That will be arranged. The fastest way to get to my estate is on the bike." He raised an eyebrow. "Unless you're afraid to be that close to me again?"

She tossed back her hair with a deliberate casualness that didn't fool him for a second. "Don't be ridiculous."

"Good." He rose from his chair, reaching out for her hand. "Let's go."

She stared at him for a moment, her eyes wide as the sea, then with obvious reluctance gave him her hand. It felt small and cool in his own. "Fine," she said with a sigh. "Take me."

Oh, he intended to.

But she hung back, glancing back at the table. "What about the ring? Are you just going to leave it?"

Nikos shrugged. Since the jewelry hadn't worked, it was of no further use to him. All he could think about now was that her skin felt warmer by the second. He yearned to touch her all over, to feel her hands on his body.

"Is everything all right, Mr. Stavrakis?" the waiter asked nervously behind him. "I hope there was no problem with your dinner?"

His eyes focused on the young waiter who'd served Anna earlier. He looked scared, holding a platter of dirty dishes on his shoulder.

"Your tip's on the table," Nikos replied abruptly. Then he turned back to push Anna out of the restaurant.

He heard a loud gasp, and the clatter of dishes falling to the floor as the waiter saw the ring, but he didn't wait for thanks. All he could think was that he had to get Anna home and in his bed. Within minutes they were roaring down the highway on his motorcycle.

The moon was full, casting shadows over the sagebrush and distant mountains. Anna clung to Nikos on the back of the motorcycle, her dark hair whipping wildly around her face as they sped across the wide moonlit desert.

She tightened her grip on his narrow waist, pressing her body against his. He was driving like a bullet, and the wind was cold against her bare arms and back. But that wasn't the reason she was shivering.

She was burning like a furnace, lit up from within.

She knew why Nikos was driving down the highway as if all the demons of hell were in hot pursuit. She'd seen it in his dark eyes. She'd felt it in the way he'd touched her. In the way he'd taken possession of her hand and pulled her from the casino.

He was going to make love to her. Until she couldn't see straight. Until she couldn't think.

Until she agreed to marry him.

She felt beads of sweat break out on her forehead, instantly wiped away by the cool desert wind.

It terrified her how badly she wanted him in return. She was barely keeping herself in check. She was afraid she'd give in.

To sleeping with him.

To everything.

Had anyone ever defied Nikos for long? Was it even possible?

She shivered again.

"Cold, my sweet?" Nikos asked in a husky voice as they pulled into the ten-car garage. Turning off the engine, he set the kickstand and gently took her hand, pulling her off the bike. He ran his fingers down the inside of her wrist as he pulled her close. "You won't be cold for long."

She backed away. "I—need to go feed Misha," she gasped out, and hurried down the hall. She was surprised and relieved beyond measure when he didn't follow her.

Afterward, as she closed the nursery door, leaving a well-fed slumbering baby behind her, she was just congratulating herself on escaping her fate when she heard his voice.

"I shouldn't have called you a bad mother. It's not true."

She whirled around to see Nikos step forward in the moonlit hallway, his face half hidden by shadows.

Gulping a breath, she looked down at the floor. "Nikos!"

He came closer and lightly brushed her wind-tangled hair off her shoulders. "I'm sorry I said it. You are good with him."

She knew that his brief kindness was part of his plan to wear her down, but unfortunately it was working. Those were words she'd been so desperate to hear, especially from him.

Damn! Biting her lip, she threw a look of longing at the guest bedroom the housekeeper had assigned her. It was only ten feet down the hall, but it might as well have been a million miles away as he took her in his arms.

He stared at the way her teeth rubbed against her lower lip. "You're so beautiful," he whispered, lightly tracing his finger against her cheek. "And so wild. So much passion behind that prim, dignified secretary. For all those years I never knew."

She started to tremble. She had to get out of here. She had to escape. She was already perilously close to giving in.

Swallowing, she tried to pick a fight. "Where's Lindsey tonight?"

"I have no idea. I fired her."

"You did—what?"

"She was never my lover, Anna. She fed you lies out of some deluded hope that she might be someday. But she was never my type."

"What's your type?" she retorted feebly, trying to hide her shock about Lindsey.

He blinked, then shook his head, giving her a predatory smile. "Arrogant Russian-born women with black hair, cat-shaped eyes and a tart mouth." He leaned forward to breathe in her hair, whispering in her ear. "I remember the sweet taste of you. Tart and sweet all over, Anna…"

She struggled not to remember, not to feel anything as his voice washed over her senses. "Lindsey really wasn't your lover?"

"Since that first night we were together you've been the only one." He ran his finger gently along her lips. "You're the mother of my child. I need you, Anna. In my home. In my bed."

Oh, my God. She was dizzy with longing, unable to speak.

"You are meant to be my wife." He kissed her softly on the forehead, her cheeks. "It is fate."

"But I—I don't want you," she managed, her heart threatening to jump out of her ribcage.

"Prove it," he whispered. Encircling her body with his strong arms, he slowly traced his hand down her bare back. She could feel the warmth of his skin, the strength of his hand.

"I don't," she insisted, but her voice was so weak that even she didn't believe it.

He backed her up against the wall between a large plant and a Greek statue in the wide, dark hallway. "Are you sure?"

The only thing of which she was sure was that the strain of not reaching for him was causing her physical pain. She flattened her trembling palms against the wall as he gently ran his hand through her tangled dark hair. His fingers brushed against the sensitive flesh of her earlobe. He traced lightly down her neck.

"I always get what I want, and I've never wanted any woman like I want you…"

Lowering his mouth to hers, he kissed her. His lips was gentle and oh, so seductive. Pressing her hands against his chest, she willed herself to resist. To remember the cruel way he'd humiliated her before.

I won't give in this time. I won't…

But even as she made token resistance she felt her body surrender. Her head leaned back as his tongue teased her, as his lips seared her own. She felt her mind, soul, everything float away until only longing was left.

"No!" With her last bit of will-power she pushed him away. She tried to push past him toward her room, but he blocked her. She stumbled over her high-heeled sandals, kicking them off as she turned and ran down the hall. He pursued her, as single-minded as a wolf stalking a deer. She raced outside, banging the door behind her.

In the courtyard, dark clouds had spread across the sky, and she could smell coming rain. Silver threads of moonlight laced the sky, barely holding back the storm.

Barefoot, Anna tripped across the mosaic tiles of the courtyard, skirting the edge of the pool's shimmering water. Her pale skin glowed in the moonlight as she ran beneath the dark shadows of palm trees.

Nikos caught her in front of the enormous Moroccan fountain, his arms wrapping around her from behind.

"I need you, Anna," he said huskily in her ear, holding her body against his own. "And you need me. Don't deny it."

Kissing her neck from behind, he ran his hands over her, cupping her breasts in the suede.

Sucking in her breath, she whirled to face him. Angry words fell unspoken as she saw his face. His handsome, strong face, made somehow even more masculine with the dark bristles of a five o'clock shadow on his chin. In the snug black T-shirt and dark jeans he didn't look like a billionaire tycoon. He looked like a biker, dangerous and dark, and a devil in bed.

He was right. She wanted him.

Needed him.

Could so easily love him…

"I can't," she gasped aloud.

"Can't?" He held her even tighter.

In spite of her resolve, honesty poured out of her. "I can't fight you anymore…"

His sensual lips curved into a smile as he reached his hand behind her head and pulled her into a hot, hard kiss. She returned the kiss hungrily, tasting blood in the intensity of their mutual need. His blood? Hers? She didn't care. All she knew was that she'd been denied his touch for too long. If he stopped kissing her now she would die.

She wanted to possess him as thoroughly and savagely as he'd possessed her soul…

She pressed her hands against his back, desperate to pull him closer, but it wasn't enough. She brought her hands between them, beneath his shirt, running her hands up his taut belly. She heard him gasp as she explored the trail of hair up his chest, feeling the hard planes of his torso. He'd always been strong, but his muscles were bigger now, harder than they'd ever been. And more…

"What's this?" she murmured aloud, but didn't wait for an answer. She yanked on the black T-shirt, and he let her pull it off his body. She lightly traced a hard ridge across his naked collarbone, then found another one over his ribs.

"You have new scars," she whispered.

He shrugged, a deceptively careless gesture. "I worked some aggression out in the boxing ring while you were gone."

"I'm sorry—"

"I'm not. I'm stronger now. No one will ever have to do my fighting for me again."

Unlike most rich men, she thought in a daze. Unlike Victor.

Nikos ran his hands up and down her halter top, caressing the soft suede, pressing her breasts upwards until they threatened to spill over. He reached beneath the top, cupping and weighing their fullness, then bent to nuzzle between them. The dark stubble of his chin was rough against her tender skin, sending prickles all over her body as he licked his way slowly to her neck. He sucked at the crook of her shoulder, causing pain and pleasure and a mark of possession.

She moaned softly, arching into him. He pushed her back roughly against the tiled wall of the courtyard. Her eyelids fluttered, and as if in a dream she saw the splash of colorful tile in the moonlight, heard the burble of the stone fountain.

She couldn't let this happen…

She couldn't stop herself from letting it happen…

Dazed and unsteady, she threw her arms back against the wall for support. He pressed his hands on the small of her back, pulling her closer, tighter. His naked chest pressed against her, the hard muscles of his arms wrapped around her bare arms. Their legs were tangled as she felt the naked skin of his taut belly against her own. He kissed her hard, running his hands through her hair.

He ran his hands along the sides of her jeans. Jeans! She cursed the choice. Why hadn't she worn a skirt? He grabbed her backside, lifting her up so she could wrap her legs around him. She could feel how hard he was, how ready for her. She wanted him to take her here, now, against the wall, before she had time to think.

"God, I want you," he whispered. "For the last year you're the only woman I've been able to think about. Just you. Only you."

She took a deep breath. "Then take me."

There. She'd said it. Right or wrong, she'd dared to admit what they both already knew: she wanted him. Her cheeks felt hot; she felt like a hoyden. She took a deep breath. "But please be gentle. My—my doctor said the first time I had sex after the baby might feel like…like I was a virgin. It might hurt."

He pulled back abruptly, giving her a searing look. "I would never hurt you, *agape mou*."

At that moment she believed him. "I know."

But he still hesitated, looking troubled. She realized that he was holding himself back because he didn't want to cause her pain. He still cared about her. For the first time she felt the magnitude of her own power over him, and it thrilled her.

She smiled up at him, tracing the beauty of his slightly crooked nose with her fingertip, touching his bare scars. He was a warrior, fierce and powerful, and frightening in his beauty.

But, powerful as he was, she realized she could match his fire.

Bracing her hands on his shoulders, she unwrapped her legs from his body. Backing away, she reached behind her and untied her halter top. It fell into her hands, leaving her upper body naked. Moonlight briefly drenched her skin in an opalescent glow the color of pearls, then disappeared behind the dark clouds that were rapidly covering the sky.

She stood in front of him in the semidarkness, straight and tall. She'd never been this brave before. Even during the months of their affair she'd always let him take the lead. Nervous at her own daring, she looked into his face.

His expression was strained. With a low growl he lifted her back into his arms, pressing her against the wall. The feeling of his skin against her own, without the halter top to separate them, was exquisite. But it wasn't enough—still not nearly enough.

Clasping her wrists tightly in one massive hand, he pulled her arms over her head, kissing down her body as he moved his other hand between her legs. Her earlier fear of pain was already forgotten as she moved against him, wanting to feel more. To feel *him*. Above her, she could hear the howl of rising wind, and she felt small drops of rain against her overheated skin. Her hair whipped wildly as she leaned her head back, hardly able to breathe, out of her mind with longing.

"I take it all back," she gasped. "Don't be gentle. Don't make me wait. Take me now."

He gave her a lazy smile as his fingers caressed her through her jeans. "You want me to take you here? Against the wall?"

"Yes. And I don't give a damn who might see." She

only knew that if he kept stroking her through her jeans she was going to come any second.

But he didn't make a move to pull off her jeans. Instead he kept stroking her, moving his chest against hers, plundering her mouth with his own.

"Stop," she panted. Pushing his hand away, she strained toward him, her hands fumbling at his zipper. "I want to feel you inside me—"

"No." He grabbed her hands. "Wait."

A roll of thunder shattered the clouds and cold rain began to fall, splattering across the courtyard and pool. Wind howled across the desert, rattling the palm trees high above them as they stared at each other.

"I want you. But—" He blinked, as if trying to clear his mind of a fog, shaking his head like a wolf scattering water from his fur. "This is a mistake. When I make love to you again it will be in a bed…"

She saw a glimmer of hope. "My bedroom is—"

"As my wife," he finished.

They stared at each other in the moonlight, whipped by wind and hard rain. Anna was suddenly aware that she was standing half naked, with cold, hard rain sleeting down her bare breasts.

She'd just thrown herself at him.

And he'd refused her. Her cheeks flushed with shame.

"If you wait for me to marry you, you'll wait forever," she retorted, blinking back angry tears. He'd only been trying to prove his power over her, and she'd fallen for it yet again. She reached down to the tiled floor and snatched up her halter top, now ruined in the rain. Her hands shook as she tied the strings in back. Her teeth chattered as she said, "Just being your mistress nearly killed me. I will never be your wife, Nikos. Never."

Beneath the darkness of the desert storm she could barely see his face for shadows. But his voice was low and dangerous, resonant with the certainty that only came from power. "We'll see."

The next morning, Nikos growled at the housekeeper's cheery greeting as she brought his breakfast to the table. She set down a cup of strong Greek coffee and a plate of eggs, bacon and toast, then left. He stared blankly at the morning editions of the *Wall Street Journal* and the local *Review-Journal* and cursed himself for a fool.

He hadn't slept all night, and it was his own damned fault.

It was not in his nature to be patient, but he'd left Anna in the courtyard and gone to his bedroom alone. Where he'd tossed and turned until dawn.

He swore softly to himself. If he'd just made love to Anna last night, perhaps he'd already be free of this spell.

He took a gulp of the hot coffee. He'd need all the help he could get to make it through the day. He had to secure a new secretary to replace Lindsey, the negotiations for the land lease bid for his new casino resort project in Singapore were at a critical juncture, and all he could think about was getting Anna in bed. He was so wound up he couldn't see straight.

He was off his game. Just when his business urgently needed his attention. It was intolerable.

And the worst thing was he had no idea how to convince Anna to be his wife. It was the best thing for everyone. Damn it, why couldn't she see that?

He'd already reasoned with her. Fired Lindsey. Bought her a two-hundred-thousand-dollar ring. He'd offered Anna wealth and the protection of his name, and she'd thrown them back in his face.

Even seducing her hadn't made her agree to his proposal. For a man accustomed to negotiation, he was in a tough spot. What was left to offer?

"More toast, Mr. Stavrakis?"

He growled in reply. Accustomed to his moods, the housekeeper gave him a cheerful nod. "By the way, thank you for hiring Mrs. Burbridge. She's already popular among the staff. And such a sweet baby you have too, sir, if you don't mind me saying so."

"Thank you," he bit out, then picked up the nearest paper to signal the end of the conversation. After the housekeeper had left he took several bites of food, then threw his paper down and went to look for Anna.

He found her at the pool, and watched her for several seconds from the doorway before she saw him.

She was in the water, holding Michael. The baby was laughing and splashing as she skimmed him through the water in the warm morning sun. Anna held him close, pointing out things in the courtyard. "And those are palm trees, and a fountain. That's the blue sky, and the water is blue too. It's going to be hot today," she said to the baby, smiling. "So different from your great-grandmama's old palace, isn't it, Misha?"

Nikos envied her playful ease with the baby. He felt like an outsider looking at a loving family. It wasn't supposed to be this way. Having a child was his chance for a fresh start. To have a family of his own. To be the father he himself had never had. Damn it, how had everything gone so wrong?

It should have made him resent her, reminded him to hate her, but instead he felt only envy and a whisper of loneliness. Anna was simply in the pool doing nothing, splashing and wading, but he could tell she was having the time of her life because she loved just spending time with their child.

He'd been wrong to think about taking Michael away from her. Even if he'd been cruel enough to do it, Anna never would have accepted it. She would have fought him all the way. She had absolute loyalty and a single-minded devotion to those she loved.

His eyes went wide.

That was how he could get Anna to marry him.

Not jewelry. Not money. Not even sex.

Love. Love was the glue that would bind her.

He had to make Anna fall in love with him—fall so hard and fast that she'd not only marry him but would spend the rest of her life trying to get his love in return.

Which, of course, he wouldn't give her. He wasn't a fool. Loving her would make him weak when he most needed to be strong. How could he guard his family, protect them as they deserved, if his judgment was impaired? He'd never allowed himself to love anyone, and he never intended to.

But her loving him—that was something else. She had a character that was born for devotion. If she loved him it would ensure her loyalty for a lifetime. It would keep his son safe with a loving mother, and he'd be protected from stepfathers like Sinistyn.

It couldn't be that hard to make Anna love him, he reasoned. She'd said she loved him before, though he hadn't realized it at the time. All he needed to do was repeat those same conditions and she would do so again.

But she must never suspect what he was doing. She had to think she was falling for him of her own free will.

He narrowed his eyes, watching as Anna laughed with their baby, splashing in the pool, tilting her lovely pale face back to drink in the warm Nevada sun.

What carrot could he dangle in front of her to convince her to be with him and spend unguarded time together?

What if he allowed her to work as his secretary again? Just for a few days? Of course it would be temporary. And, hell, he'd actually be grateful for Anna's help in selecting a new secretary. Maybe she could even help polish the negotiations for the Singapore deal.

But it wouldn't take long. A week, maybe just a few days of working together. He'd put on the charm. He'd spout nonsense about his *feelings*, if that was what it took. He'd wine her and dine her until she surrendered her body and soul.

And what a body. Her skin was pale as a Russian

winter, but she looked sexy as hell, barely decent beneath a tiny string bikini that matched the alluring turquoise of the water. She'd certainly never worn anything like *that* when she was his mistress. She'd never flaunted her curves, never tried once to tease him. She hadn't had to; she'd driven him wild even as a buttoned-up secretary who wore her hair in a bun and covered up her body with elegant loose-fitting suits.

But who was this siren in her place? String bikini today. Tight jeans and clinging halter top yesterday. Had Anna really changed so much?

He saw her give a worried glance at the sun and, cuddling the baby to her chest, she climbed up the wide pool steps. She pulled sunscreen out of the old, frayed diaper bag sitting on the stone table near the fountain. Sitting back on a nearby lounge chair, she sat the chubby baby down on her flat belly and playfully tickled him while slathering him with sunscreen.

She reached for a wide-brimmed hat on the edge of the stone table. Her nearly nude body stretched beneath the bikini, revealing the side swell of her breasts.

Mrs. Burbridge nearly ran into him as she hurried around the courtyard doorway.

"Oh! Excuse me, sir."

He'd been so intent on watching Anna that he hadn't heard the plump woman come up behind him. He straightened. "My fault, Mrs. Burbridge."

"I was just going to ask Mrs. Stav—er, Miss Rostoff—" she flushed with embarrassment as she tripped over the name "—if she wanted me to take the baby inside. She didn't sleep well last night, so I thought perhaps she'd like a bit of a rest."

"She didn't sleep well?"

"She has the room next to mine. I heard her pacing. Jet lag, I suppose, poor dear."

So Anna had slept as badly as he had. Nikos would be willing to bet money it hadn't been jet lag that had troubled her all night.

His lips curved up in a smile. *Perfect.* It was all coming together. By the end of the week—by the end of the day, if he was lucky—Mrs. Burbridge would never have to trip over Anna's name again. She would be Mrs. Stavrakis.

Anna was barely back in the pool with Misha when she saw Mrs. Burbridge standing by the water's edge. But it wasn't the appearance of the Scotswoman that set her hackles on edge. It was the man behind her, who was staring at her like an ant under a microscope, as if he'd never seen a woman in a swimsuit before.

"Would you like me to take the bairn, Miss Rostoff?" Mrs. Burbridge asked. "I thought you might like a wee rest."

Since it was only ten o'clock in the morning, she was sure the "wee rest" was Nikos's idea. He wanted to get her alone, so he could finish his seduction and convince her to be his bride.

Not in this lifetime.

Anna turned to wade in the other direction, holding the baby close as if she feared the older woman might fling herself in the pool, orthopedic shoes and all, and wrestle Misha away. "No, thank you, Mrs. Burbridge. We're happy as we are."

She waited for Nikos to demand that she give up the baby, but to her surprise he didn't. "Obviously she's not tired," she heard him tell the nanny. "I think we'll just spend some time together as a family."

Anna heard Mrs. Burbridge leave and looked back, hoping that Nikos had left too. No such luck. He was standing by the pool, watching her with an inscrutable expression. His presence was like a dark cloud over the sun. It made her tense, remembering how easily she'd almost given herself to him last night, how much she still wanted to feel him inside her. The argument between longing and fury had kept her up all night. Twice she'd nearly weakened and gone to his room. It was only by the sheerest self-preservation that she hadn't woken up this morning in his bed, with a big engagement ring on her finger.

At least then she'd also have woken up with a big smile on her face. She shook the thought away.

"Well?" she said, giving him her haughtiest stare— the one her mother had used to give to other people's servants when they sneered at their family as "charity cases" and purposefully ruined their meals or their laundry behind their employers' backs. Until Anna was eighteen, when her father had returned the family to New York and gone into business with Victor, their life had been full of insult and insecurity.

And after that Victor had had power over them. That

was why she would never allow herself to be dependent upon someone else for her livelihood again. Better to starve in a garret and have her pride.

At least that was what she'd thought before she became a mother. Now she wasn't so sure. What was her own pride compared to the safety and well-being of her child?

"What do you want?" she demanded irritably.

Instead of answering, Nikos sat down on the tiled edge of the pool. He folded his legs Indian-style, looking strangely at ease, almost boyish. Her eyebrows rose at the sight of Nikos, in his elegant Italian wool trousers and crisp white shirt, sitting on the dusty tile floor of the courtyard. "I want you to teach me how to be a parent."

Her jaw dropped ever so slightly. "What do you mean?"

He glanced at Misha. "You know I never had a father. Not a real one, at any rate. I have no idea how to be one. I'm afraid to hold my own son."

Anna waited for him to point out that it was all her fault for stealing Misha for the first four months of his life, but again Nikos surprised her. He said instead, in a tone that was almost humble, "I need you to teach me how to be a father."

It's a trick, she warned herself, but for the life of her she couldn't see how. She licked her lips nervously. She glanced at the precious babe in her arms. He needed a good father, and, although she was far from a parenting expert, she was at least an expert on her own baby. How could she refuse?

"I suppose I could try," she said reluctantly.

"So you agree?"

"When do you want to start?"

"Now."

"Get a swimsuit, then."

"That would take too long." In a fluid motion, he pulled his shirt over his head and tossed it aside. Kicking off his shoes, he looked at her, and she suddenly realized what he was going to do.

"You can't be serious!"

"Anna, you know I'm *always* serious," he said, and jumped into the pool, trousers and all.

She turned away, protecting the baby from the enormous splash as he landed in the deep end of the pool. When he rose from the water his hair was plastered to his head. He spouted water like a fish, and his expensive Italian trousers were almost certainly ruined, but he was *laughing*.

Oh, my God. The sound of his laugh. She hadn't heard that for a long, long time. Nikos's laugh, so hearty and bold and rare, like a fine Greek wine, had first made her love him.

He swam over towards the shallow end, until his feet touched the bottom, and then he walked towards her, parting the water like a Greek god. He was six feet two inches, and the water only lapped his waistband when he reached her. His muscular torso glistened in the hot sun, and rivulets of water ran down his body. She nervously licked her lips as he put one hand on her bare shoulder and with the other gently caressed their baby's head.

"Will you show me how to hold him?"

She carefully set Misha in his arms, showing him how to hold the baby close to his chest.

"Hi," he said, looking down at the baby in his arms. "I know you've never had a father. This is my first time being one. We'll learn how to do this together."

Carefully, he moved deeper into the pool, until the baby laughed at the pleasurable feeling of the water against his skin. Nikos joined in his laughter as Misha joyfully splashed the water with his pudgy hands.

He kissed the baby's downy head and whispered, so low that Anna almost didn't hear, "I will always be here to help you swim, Michael."

Anna watched with her heart in her throat. She'd thought she was in danger before. But now, watching him with their son, holding him tenderly, she saw in Nikos everything she'd ever wanted. A strong man who wasn't afraid to be playful.

This was the father she wanted for her child.

The husband she'd always dreamed of for herself.

She tried to push those troublesome thoughts away. It wasn't the real Nikos, she told himself. He was trying to trick her, to lure her in for the sake of his revenge. He wouldn't stop until he'd crushed her, heart and soul.

For the rest of the morning she waited for Nikos to revert to his usual arrogant, cold personality, but he never did.

They were like a happy family. It left her amazed. And shaken.

When she left the pool to go feed and change Misha

for his nap, he climbed out behind her. The ruined Italian trousers dripped and sloshed water behind him. She glanced at them with a rueful smile. "Sorry about your pants."

"I'm not." He gave her a grin. He looked relaxed and something else…contented? Had she ever seen him look that way before? "Besides, I can get more. I haven't had that much fun in ages. I felt like a kid again."

She snorted. "If it was that great, maybe next time in the pool I'll wear a snowsuit."

"Please don't," he said lazily. "I like the bikini."

The look he cast over her made her suddenly feel warm all over, in a way that had nothing to do with the hot desert sun.

"You didn't like my outfit last night."

"That was different," he said. "That was for another man."

She waited for him to lash into her accusingly, demanding that she never see Sinistyn again, but he just turned away to head back into the house. "I'm going to slip into something a little less wet," he said with a wink. "After Michael's asleep come see me in the office, will you? I have a proposal."

A proposal? Thank heavens, she thought as she hurried back to the nursery with her cranky, yawning baby. Nikos's behavior had been starting to confuse her. But she knew that as soon as she met him in the office he would start tossing out demands. He'd try to kiss her senseless until she agreed to his marriage proposal.

That she could deal with. It was his new playfulness,

his kindness and love for his son, that she didn't know how to handle.

She showed up at the office with a T-shirt and shorts over her bikini, ready for battle. She was so ready, in fact, that she could hardly wait for him to take her in his arms. All the kisses in the world wouldn't convince her to marry him, but since she'd managed to get through last night unscathed, she was willing—no, eager—to let him try…

But he didn't touch her. The enormous mahogany desk that filled his home office had a light lunch spread at one end, while he sat working at the other, surrounded by piles of disorganized papers that were also stacked on the floor. He somehow managed to ignore the mess, focusing on his laptop.

He was dressed now, in a T-shirt and casual button-down shirt. He greeted her with a smile and nodded toward the food. "I had the housekeeper bring lunch. I figured you'd be hungry."

"You figured right," she said, and went straight for the gourmet sandwiches and the fruit and cheese tray. Nursing left her hungrier than she'd ever been before, and thirstier too. She gulped down some sparkling water. She waited, but he still seemed intent on his laptop. She cleared her throat.

He looked up, as if he'd forgotten she was there.

"Um…why did you want me to join you here?" she asked, confused at his behavior. "You said you wanted to ask me something?"

"Oh. Right. I need your help. I'm closing my bid on

the land lease for a new casino in Singapore, and since I fired Lindsey I have no executive assistant."

A thrill went through Anna. He wanted her back! She'd always taken such pride in her work, and she and Nikos had connected creating L'Hermitage. She tried to temper her growing hope. "But what about Margaret? Or Clementine in your New York office? They could quickly come up to speed."

"I need them where they are. The New York office are up to their necks getting zoning approval for the Battery co-op. And Margaret has her hands full with L'Hermitage. I need to hire someone new as my personal assistant, and I'll be leaving for Singapore in ten days. I need your help."

Her heart started to beat, thump, thump. Returning to work for Stavrakis Resorts would be a dream come true. She wondered if the baby would like traveling around the world.

"All right," she said, trying to hide her elation. "Since you need me."

"I was hoping you'd say that." He pushed a piece of paper down the desk.

To her confusion, Anna saw that it was a résumé. "What's this?"

"The first candidate." He looked at her with his velvety brown eyes, and a warm smile traced his lips. "To replace you."

CHAPTER SIX

ANNA felt as if she'd just been sucker-punched.

"Replace me?" She thrust the résumé back at him, as if it burned her fingers. "Why would I help you replace me? This job was my life. Why would I help you give it away? I'm not going to lift a finger for you."

"Good point," he said briskly, then pushed another official document toward her. "Would this convince you?"

She picked up the attached papers, frowning. "Another résumé will hardly—"

But, as she read the first words on the page, her jaw fell open and she collapsed back against the hard wooden chair.

"It's a custody agreement," she gasped when she could speak.

"Yes," he said pleasantly.

She fumbled through the pages, but her hands were shaking and the paperclip fell to the floor. Bending to pick it up, she looked up at him. "You're going to give me joint custody?"

"Call it incentive."

"What do you want in return?" she said guardedly.

"I'll sign the custody agreement if you help me find a good executive assistant within ten days."

She stared at him. "That's all? I just have to help you find a new secretary and you'll give me joint custody of Misha? You'll let me leave?"

He gave a graceful shrug. "I'm a desperate man. I need this settled by the time I leave for Singapore."

She could hardly believe her ears. It was way too good to be true. "I thought you said you were going to make me suffer for betraying you?"

"As I said yesterday, I've come to appreciate your love and care for my son."

Yeah, right. "There's something you're not telling me."

"So suspicious," he said, then closed his laptop with a sigh. "You will, of course, agree never to see Victor Sinistyn again."

She nearly laughed aloud. At last it made sense. Perhaps he did want her help finding a new secretary, but it was Victor that really worried him. Her plan had worked better than she'd ever dared dream.

She opened her mouth to tell him she'd be perfectly happy to cross Victor's name permanently off her Christmas card list, but closed it as another thought occurred to her.

What if Nikos changed his mind before she found him a new assistant and he signed the custody agreement? If she agreed to stop seeing Victor she'd lose her only hold on Nikos. She couldn't play out her hand so easily.

"I'm not sure I can do that." She tilted her head, as if considering his offer. "Victor is a hard man to forget."

She saw a glint of something hard and flinty in Nikos's eyes, then it was veiled beneath a studiously careless expression. "It's your choice, of course."

"Whether I'm friends with Victor?"

"Whether you want joint custody of our son."

Hardly able to believe her own daring, she said, "Of course I do. But I'll need more than your signature on a custody agreement to give up a man who might be the love of my life."

His eyes were decidedly hard now, glittering like coal turning to diamonds under pressure. "What do you want?"

"You want a new secretary to replace me. Understandable. I want a new boss to replace *you*. Give me a glowing reference so I can find a good job in New York."

"I never agreed you could take our son to New York."

"What do you care? You'll be in Singapore—"

"And you'll never need to work again," he interrupted, not listening. "I will supply you with all the money you could possibly need to raise our child in comfort. Do not insult me."

"It's hardly an insult to wish to work."

"Your job now is to take care of our son."

"That's your job too, since you're his parent as well, but I haven't noticed you putting Stavrakis Resorts up for sale."

"The company is my son's legacy," he said. "I have no choice but to work."

"Neither do I."

"I will always support Michael. And you as well, for the rest of your life. I protect what is mine. You need never fear for money again."

"And my family, too? Will you support my mother and sister for all their lives as well?"

"A reasonable amount…" he started, then his gaze sharpened. "Why do you ask? Is your family in some kind of trouble?"

She really didn't want to discuss this. Backtracking furiously, she said, "I appreciate your offer of support, Nikos, I really do, but I don't want to be beholden to you for the rest of my life."

He drummed his fingers impatiently on the table. "So let me get this straight. You want our son to be raised by a nanny just so you can work as a secretary?"

"Are you implying my job is less important than yours?" she countered.

"No, I'm flat-out saying it. Stavrakis Resorts has thousands of employees around the world, all depending on the company for their salary. It's not even close to the same. In your case, I think the world can survive with one less typist."

"You know perfectly well there's more to what I do!" she said, outraged.

"Nothing in your job description could possibly be as important as—" He visibly restrained himself. He sat back in his leather chair and gave her a smile that didn't reach his eyes. "Anna, there's no reason we have to discuss this now. Until you help me find your replacement, it's all a moot point."

"I want to discuss it now," she said mutinously.

He sat in stillness, then gave a sigh. "Fine. Find me a new secretary—a good one—and I'll give you your job reference, if that's really what you want. God knows you deserve it."

"Even though I was *just a typist*?"

"You know I didn't mean that." He scowled. "Let me explain."

That surprised her. Nikos never explained, he just gave orders. "I'm listening."

Raking back his hair, he looked through the window. Outside, a gardener was riding a lawnmower across the expansive heavily watered lawn, a slash of green against barren brown mountains and harsh blue sky. "I barely saw my mother growing up. She was always working three jobs to keep a roof over our heads. By the time I was old enough to help support us she'd died. I never knew her except as a pale ghost with a broken heart."

He looked at Anna. "I never want my son, or you, to endure that kind of wretched life. I know I've given you no reason to accept anything from me, but please let me do this one thing. Let me give Michael the happy childhood I never had."

Anna swallowed. It was hard to ignore a plea like that. And harder still to ignore the pleas of her own heart. She didn't want to leave her baby all day long so she could go to work, but what choice did she have? It was either work or beg money from Nikos for the rest of her life.

But maybe it wouldn't be like that.

Stupid to even consider it. She'd trusted Nikos once before and she'd just been abandoned, fired, cheated on…

He never cheated on me, a voice whispered. *And, no matter how misguided and neanderthal his attempts were, he was only trying to keep us both comfortable and safe.*

She stomped on the thought. She wouldn't let herself weaken now and start going soft again. She wouldn't let Nikos get under her skin, no matter how vulnerable he looked asking for her help, or how warm his eyes had glowed when he'd laughed with their son. She wouldn't let herself fall back in love, no matter how wonderful he seemed to be at this moment.

She snatched the résumé back out of his hands, eager for distraction from her thoughts. "This is the job candidate you plan to interview first?"

"Yes, I thought—"

Skimming the page, she nearly jumped out of her chair. "Have you totally lost your mind? She has no secretarial experience. Her references are a strip club and—" she squinted her eyes "—a place called the Hot Mustang Ranch."

"I was trying to keep an open mind," he said defensively. "Your reference was Victor Sinistyn, but you were still the best damn secretary I've ever had."

"But there are three typos on her *résumé*. Even Lindsey wasn't this bad." She crumpled up the paper in her hands.

"There's no point even doing an interview—not unless you need an erotic dancer with bordello experience."

"Fine," he said gruffly. "I'll have her sent away. Maybe your friend Victor will hire her at one of his clubs."

He held out his hand for the paper. As their fingers touched their eyes met, and an electric shock went through her. He looked at her so hungrily. She waited for him to take her in his arms, to kiss her senseless. To reach across the mahogany desk and take what she'd been aching for him to take.

She heard him take a long, slow breath. His fingers slowly moved up her bare arm as they both leaned forward over the table.

There was a hard knock at the door, the sound of it swinging open. "Excuse me, sir, miss?"

Anna whirled around in her chair, blushing when she saw a maid standing in the doorway.

"I have standing orders not to be interrupted in my office," Nikos said in a controlled voice.

"Yes, sir. But, begging your pardon, it's Miss Rostoff who's wanted. Your sister's here, miss. She's quite agitated and said if we didn't get you she'd be calling the police and telling them you were being kept here against your will."

"Let me go!" Anna heard her sister's voice, shrill and frantic down the hall. "Get out of my way. Anna? Anna!"

Natalie pushed past the maid, nearly knocking the girl aside. Her linen shift dress was rumpled and dirty, as if it had been slept in.

She stopped abruptly when she saw Anna in her T-shirt

and shorts, sitting casually on the desk near Nikos. Natalie's jaw dropped, then her eyes blazed through her thick glasses.

"You've got some nerve," she said to Anna. "Do you have any idea what's going on? I've been calling and calling, but you never called back. I thought you were in trouble. I thought he was keeping you prisoner again. And instead I find you lazing in luxury with the man you called your deadliest enemy!"

"Excuse us," Anna said hastily, and grabbed her sister's wrist, pulling her out of the office before she could repeat any of the insulting things Anna had once said about Nikos. She couldn't risk alienating him now—not when they'd finally made a fragile peace and he was actually considering joint custody.

She dragged Natalie into her bedroom and closed the door behind her.

"You've gone back to him, haven't you?" her sister said bitterly, rubbing her wrist. "Even after all the stuff he did. Ruining Father's company! Abandoning you! Cheating on you! Firing you because you were pregnant—with his baby! That's blatant sex discrimination. You should sue."

"Natalie, I'm not going to sue the father of my child."

"Why, when he's such a monster?"

Anna took a deep breath. "I blew things out of proportion. And I just found out that what I told you about Father's company…wasn't true."

"What?"

Anna looked at her young, idealistic sister and just

couldn't bear to disillusion her by telling her about their father's embezzlement. "There were complications and problems that I didn't know about. Nikos didn't ruin the company. He was trying to save it when Father made some…bad choices."

Natalie looked at her keenly. "So if Nikos suddenly isn't so bad, why are you marrying Victor and moving to Russia?"

"What?"

"You don't know?" Staring at her in amazement, her younger sister, usually so trusting and sweet, gave a harsh laugh. "No, of course you don't. I've only left ten messages on your cellphone since yesterday. Victor Sinistyn just bought great-grandmother's palace this morning from Mother. She sold it to him for a fraction of its value—two million off our debt, plus another twenty thousand to her in cash. Which she's already spent on clothes, of course. Victor is going to raze the old palace and build something new in its place. For you."

"For me? What are you talking about?"

"Vitya always seemed so strong, so handsome. Even after he quit his partnership with Father so suddenly I thought he was kind. I flew here last night to ask him to leave the palace alone. I thought he'd listen to me." She shook her head angrily. "But he just laughed. He said that the air in Las Vegas was getting unhealthy, and that he needed to raze the palace immediately because the two of you would be moving to St. Petersburg as soon as you were married."

"That's not true!" Anna gasped. "We're not getting

married. He hasn't even proposed." *At least not lately,* she added silently.

"Well, he obviously thinks proposing is just a formality. Any reason why he'd think that?"

Anna paced across the thick blue carpet. "I've only seen him once since I got here! And even then it was only because…" Glancing right and left, as if she feared Nikos might be listening from the large walk-in closet or beneath the elegant canopied bed, Anna whispered, "Being Victor's friend is my only bargaining chip against Nikos to get joint custody. So I can leave here. So I can be free."

Natalie eyes widened, looking owlish beneath her glasses. "And you asked Vitya for help? When I went to his club I saw the kind of man he really is. He isn't our friend. If he were, he wouldn't have been loaning our parents money at that huge interest rate. I thought he was trying to help us. But now I think he only went into business with Father in the first place to be close to you. After you left to work for Nikos he dissolved the partnership and started loaning Father money instead." She took a deep breath. "I think since you wouldn't agree to marry him he's been drowning our family in debt to force your hand."

"It can't be true," Anna gasped. All right, so Victor had made advances the whole time she'd been his secretary. He'd chased off other suitors. He'd pressured her to marry him. He'd even gotten her father to try to use his influence over her. But Victor would never have deliberately hurt her family just to possess her.

Would he?

"It's the only thing that makes sense," Natalie pressed. "Why else does he keep loaning Mother money? He knows we have no way to repay it."

Anna rubbed her head wearily. "I don't know. But I'll figure it out. I'll handle this, Natalie, don't worry. As soon as I get custody of Misha I'll return to New York and find a job—"

"You still think he'll let you repay the money?" Natalie interrupted, looking at Anna as if seeing her for the first time. "If you think he's gone to all this trouble to let you set up some kind of payment plan, you're as delusional as Mother. Who's happy to take his money, by the way, because she's sure you'll marry him. Which you probably will. You always have to sacrifice yourself, don't you? Even when it does more harm than good. You'll reward him after he's destroyed our family to get his hands on you."

"You don't know that's really true!"

"I don't?" Natalie shook her head. "You need to grow up and see the real world."

Her baby sister was telling *her* to grow up? "I do see the real world—"

"My whole life I've thought you were some kind of saint, you know? Sacrificing your own future to take care of us. When I wanted to study accounting so I could get a good job to help support our family you insisted I major in art instead—"

"I knew art was your passion!" Anna said, stung.

"Maybe." Natalie snorted derisively. "But it's no way

to make a living. The truth is, you didn't *want* my help. You always have to be the one to do everything. God forbid you ever depend on someone else."

"I was trying to do the right thing for you!"

"Then why didn't you stand up to Victor ages ago and tell him to back off? Instead of running away to work for someone else? Why did you get pregnant by Nikos, then run away? Why are you still so desperate to run away from Nikos now? You're keen to stand up for others, but when it comes to yourself you just run away."

Anna stared at her, breathing heavily. "Natalie, please…" she whispered.

Natalie's eyes were hard. "You want to be strong? Fine. You got yourself in your mess. With Victor. With Nikos. Get yourself out of it. Just don't kid yourself that your choices are for us. All you've done is make things worse for *us*. Thanks. Thanks a lot."

Turning on her heel, she went for the door.

"Natalie!" She grabbed her sister's wrist. "Don't leave like this. Please."

"Let me go," Natalie said coldly. Her sister wrenched her arm away, and this time Anna released her.

After she left, Anna slowly sat down on the bed in the cool darkness of her room, still shocked by Natalie's attack. Her sister had always been the one person Anna could count on. She hadn't asked any questions when Anna had appeared on her doorstep in Russia, but had simply taken her in her arms and let her cry on her shoulder. She'd fought Nikos's armed henchmen to try to keep Misha safe.

Heartsick, Anna left her room and realized she'd blindly gone to Nikos's office to seek comfort. But his door was closed. She stared at the door, longing for him to take her in his strong arms and tell her everything would be okay. She would almost believe it if he was the one who said it. No doubt another example of her being *delusional.*

Was Natalie right?

Instead of being the one who'd saved and supported her family, had Anna been the cause of its ruin?

It was true that she'd never really stood up to Victor. He'd made passes at her, and Anna hadn't known how to deal with his flirtations, so she'd simply put up with them. She'd never told him flat-out to leave her alone. When they'd gotten to be too much, she'd run away to work for Nikos.

And as for Nikos… She'd known his faults, but she'd still fallen in love with him. She should have been more careful. Especially about jumping into his bed. What had she been thinking to allow herself to conceive a child with a man who not only wasn't her husband but didn't even love her?

The closed office door stared down at her reproachfully.

Turning away with a heavy heart, she went to the nursery, where Misha was still napping in his crib. She gently picked him up and cuddled him in the rocking chair. Tears filled her eyes as she stared out the window at the pool, where for a brief time that morning she'd felt like she was part of a happy family.

How could she fix everything she'd done wrong?

How could she make things right?

The one thing she couldn't do was ask Nikos—or anyone—for help. Natalie was right. Anna had caused this mess. She was the one who should take care of it. Alone.

Closing her eyes, she held her baby as she rocked back and forth. It was time to face reality.

Misha shouldn't suffer just because Anna had such a hard time being around his father. No matter how much she wanted to return to New York, she couldn't. She had to live close enough to Nikos that they could raise their son together. Misha deserved that much.

But she wouldn't marry Nikos either. She'd been careless enough to get pregnant, but she wouldn't make it worse by marrying him. She'd be miserable as his wife, committing herself to a man who didn't even love her.

Anna would share parenting with Nikos, but that was it. She needed her own place. Her own life. Her own job.

She sat up straight in her chair as her eyes flew open.

She'd get Nikos to rehire her.

It was the perfect solution. She'd be able to travel with him around the world, so Misha would always see them both. Plus, working as his executive assistant was not only the best job she'd ever had, he'd also paid her a high salary that would be virtually impossible to find anywhere else. Enough so that she could set up a payment plan with Victor, which she'd force him to take.

It might be difficult to see Nikos every day, no doubt watching him date other women, but she'd deal with it. She would take responsibility for the choices she'd made.

Misha gave a little sigh. Opening his dark eyes, so

much like his father's, he smiled up at her. Anna smiled back.

All she had to do was convince Nikos to hire her as his secretary—while keeping herself from falling into his arms—and everything else would fall into place.

It wouldn't be easy, but, hey—Nikos *had* asked for her help weeding out unsuitable résumés. She grinned. She'd pretend to go through them while taking over the secretarial job herself. She'd lull Nikos into complacency while she proved she could both work *and* be a good mother to his child. She'd prove to them both that she wasn't a screw-up. She'd prove she could do it all.

"What's wrong with this one?" Nikos demanded, exasperated. "Carmen Ortega has thirty years of experience working with CEOs of billion-dollar companies!"

"Those companies had shareholders," Anna said sweetly, tossing the résumé in the trash. "She's accustomed to toeing the line for many bosses instead of sticking to one. Too many cooks, you know."

No, he didn't. He had no idea what she was talking about. Nine days of looking through résumés, and Anna had found fault with every single one. But, since he'd asked specifically for her assistance, he had no choice but to continue this farce until he could get Anna to fall in love with him.

It was proving to be harder than he'd thought.

His plan had been to lure her with romantic dinners, gifts, and family outings. Instead, work had somehow taken over. She'd turned the romantic dinners into working meals, taking notes in shorthand between dainty bites of Cavaleri's pasta *primavera* and *pad thai*. When he'd given her flowers and chocolates, she'd thanked him gravely for remembering Secretaries' Day. Secretaries' Day! As if there was any damn way he'd remember some made-up holiday like that!

The family outings with baby Michael, including splashing in the pool, taking walks along the edge of the desert, and strolling through L'Hermitage, had certainly been enjoyable. Nikos had relished holding his son as they walked across the casino floor, through the Moskva Shopping Complex and into the elegant, soaring lobby of the turn-of-the-century-styled hotel. "This will all be yours someday," he'd whispered into his son's ear, and he'd been filled with pride.

But, though Anna seemed glad that he was learning to be a father, she didn't seem at all inclined to fall at his feet for that alone.

At least the time had made a difference at his home office. The piled-up papers were gone, sorted and filed. His appointments had already been reorganized to better suit his schedule, with no more double-bookings. In nine short days Anna had mended Lindsey's ineptitude with efficiency and poise.

He looked around his office. A man could get used to this, he thought with satisfaction. Then he stopped himself cold. No, he *couldn't* get used to this. He couldn't let himself. After the ten days was over Anna would return to full-time motherhood. Her place was at home, in luxury and comfort, raising their son.

It had been nice working from home for the last week, though, instead of going to his office at the casino as usual. He'd seen a lot of Michael, too, since Anna was still feeding him every three hours. She usually had him in the office with them for much of the afternoon. Right now the baby was in the nursery, taking his afternoon nap, but just a few moments ago he'd been lying on a mat on the floor, batting at the dangling toys of his playgym while he gurgled and laughed. Remembering, a smile formed on Nikos's lips.

He shook himself. What kind of work environment was this? In spite of Anna's organization, his work habits were slipping. His usual sixteen or eighteen-hour days just weren't possible when he was constantly being distracted by the laughter of his son and the gorgeous vision of Anna in a slim-fitting white shirt and black pencil skirt, crossing her killer legs while she took dictation.

No, he had to stick to his plan. Anna would be free of the burden of work, and he'd find some other secretary. He'd make do for the sake of his son having a happy childhood, and return to his eighteen-hour work days. He'd shown his son the empire that would soon be his; he couldn't slack off on the job now.

But he was leaving tomorrow. He only had tonight to make Anna fall for him before he left for Singapore, and, while he still believed he'd achieve his goal, it might be time to get creative. He'd soon have no choice but to…ugh…talk more about *feelings*. He had no idea how to do that, but he'd improvise. How hard could it be? He'd talk about his childhood. Didn't women swoon over stories of poverty and misery?

"What are you doing?" he asked, suddenly distracted by the vision of Anna's sweet backside in the form-fitting black skirt as she knelt near the trash can and leaned forward on her hands. Wild images went through him.

"This must have bounced off the rim." She picked up the crumpled résumé from the floor, then spotted something behind the can. Nikos groaned inwardly as she saw the pale blue envelope that he'd tossed there early this morning.

Leaning back on her haunches, she picked it up and read the envelope. "It's postmarked from Greece."

Nikos grabbed a new résumé. "Have you looked at this one?"

She refused to be distracted, and held the blue envelope a little higher. "When did you get this letter?"

"Yesterday," he said, grinding his teeth.

She pushed back a long tendril that had escaped from her sleek chignon. "It hasn't been opened, but it was in the trash."

"And your point is?"

"Aren't you going to read it?"

"I think my actions are self-explanatory."

"But if your father's widow wrote all the way from Greece to try to mend the breach in your family…"

"There is no breach, because there is no family," he said shortly. "My father meant nothing to me, and now he's dead, so why should I care about his widow? She can write me or not. That is her choice. I'm perfectly capable of throwing her letters in the trash without your advice."

He still remembered all too well the first letter he'd received from the Greek woman. She'd broken the news of his father's death, and informed him that he'd had left Nikos a share in his shipping business—the same shipping business that Nikos had tried to crush as an adult. Worse, she'd told him that his father had been the secret investor who had helped Nikos create Stavrakis Resorts. His father had been the one to help Nikos build his very first hotel.

Shaken, Nikos had still refused to go to the funeral, or meet his half-siblings. He'd also refused the shares in the company. He hadn't wanted any part of the family who'd been more important to his father than he and his mother had been.

But it was the kindness in her letter that had shocked him the most. She'd been so gentle, when he'd expected only hate. The confusion and pain had driven him to Anna's house. He'd instinctively sought her comfort, her arms, her bed, and they'd conceived Michael...

Anna gave him a piercing turquoise glance, as if she guessed his thoughts. "But how can you still hate your father now that you know that he helped you?"

"If I'd known he was the investor behind the venture capital firm that financed my first hotel, I would have tossed the money back in his face."

"But—"

"He was a married man when he seduced my mother. He got her pregnant, then sent her packing to New York. The man is nothing to me."

"But your stepmother—"

"Don't ever call her that again."

"Your—your father's widow said he tried to send you money every month of your childhood. Your mother was the one who always sent it back."

Yes, he remembered what the Greek woman had said—that his father had always loved Nikos, that he'd tried to visit and send child support but his proud mother had refused. She'd even said that his father hadn't wanted his mother to go to New York, that he'd been heartbroken when she'd left. She'd said his mother was the one who had refused to let him see his son.

Nikos didn't know who to believe.

His mother, of course, he told himself furiously. She had died taking care of him. She deserved his loyalty.

The last thing Nikos wanted to do was read another of the Greek woman's letters. The past was dead and gone. Better to let it remain buried.

Unfortunately, Anna didn't see it that way. Her lips pressed in a determined line. "I'm going to read the letter."

He grabbed her hand as she reached for the letter opener on his desk. "You're quick to arrange my family affairs. Is it to avoid dealing with your own?"

She hesitated. "What do you mean?"

"Why did your sister come here? You've evaded the question for over a week. I'd like an answer."

She tugged on her hand, but he held her fast. "It's nothing," she mumbled. "A family quarrel."

"Does it have anything to do with Victor Sinistyn?"

She pulled away with a savage force that he hadn't

expected. "Just stay out of it! I don't need your pity and I don't need your help. I can handle it on my own—"

She grabbed at the letter opener with a trembling hand, plunging the sharp edge of the blade into the side of the blue envelope with far too much vigor. It sliced her palm, and she squelched a scream, holding out her bleeding hand.

"Let me see your hand," Nikos demanded.

She turned her face away in a fruitless attempt to hide her tears. He was relieved that she didn't resist as he gently took her hand. Blood from the cut smudged against the cuff of his shirt as he narrowly examined the wound.

"I don't think you'll need stitches." He'd been hurt enough times while sparring in his boxing club to be a pretty good judge. "Let's just clean it in case of infection."

He led her into the adjoining bathroom, and she followed him, seemingly in a daze. She winced as he placed her hand under the running water. He dried it off softly with a thick white cotton handtowel.

"This might sting a little," he said, before he applied the antiseptic he kept in the cabinet for any injuries he got working out at the club.

She closed her eyes. His hand tightened over her fingers and he felt a strangely agonizing beat of his heart that he was hurting her, even though it was for her own good.

He placed the small bandage over the cut. "All done."

She opened her eyes. "Thank you." She started to pull away, but he stopped her.

"Anna, tell me what hold Sinistyn has got over you."

"He doesn't."

"You're a terrible liar."

"I don't need your charity, and I don't want your help," she said. "It's my family's private business." But even as she spoke the words he could see the tremor of her swanlike throat, the nervous flutter of her dark lashes.

"Not if it affects my son."

Her eyes went wide. "You think I would endanger Misha?"

He glowered at her silently until he saw her blush. Good. Let her remember her worldwide travels to unheated ramshackle apartments on her own.

"Go to hell," she said, and left him. But she'd barely gone three steps back into his office before he caught her unhurt hand.

"Tell me, or I'll beat it out of Sinistyn. Or maybe I'll just ask Cooper to track down Natalie. I doubt she's gone far."

"Please don't." She lowered her gaze to her clasped hands, then sank slowly into the hard wooden chair by his desk. "All right. I'll tell you. We're in debt."

"How much?"

She took a deep breath, still unable to meet his eyes. "It was six million, but now it's four." She suddenly gave a hysterical laugh and leaned forward, rubbing her temples. "It's at a thirty-five percent interest rate and compounding daily. That's why we were at my great-grandmother's palace, trying to get it into decent shape to find a buyer. But the palace needs a fortune in renovations to make it livable."

"You should have asked me for the money."

"You think I'd sell myself for a palace?"

"Anna!"

"Thank you for your kind offer, but we found a buyer already."

"For the palace, or for you?" he asked, trying to spur her into energy. Anything to make her eyes look less dead and defeated than they did at this moment. But she didn't even rise to his bait.

"Both, I think," she said dully. "Victor bought the palace from my mother for two million dollars. That's why we only owe him four million instead of six. He's planning to raze the palace and build a new house as a wedding present to me."

"What?" he exploded.

"Victor has wanted me for a long time." Rubbing the back of her neck wearily, she rose from the chair and started to pace. "He's been lending my parents money over the years because he knew that eventually we'd default. I think it was his way to…to back me into a corner."

Rage went through Nikos. Looking at the circles under her eyes, he wanted to rip the other man apart. "I'll kill him."

She shook her head. "No. I can handle him. I'll talk to Victor, make him understand that I don't love him and I'll never be his wife. If you want to help me, there's just one thing you can do. One thing that would really, really help me."

"What's that?" Nikos asked, relieved at her admission that she had no intention of marrying Victor Sinistyn.

She looked at him with a painful expression of hope in her lovely almond-shaped eyes. "Hire me back as your secretary so I can pay back our family's debt."

"I told you. You don't have to worry about the debt. I'll handle it," Nikos said. *And I'll start by destroying Sinistyn,* he vowed privately.

"Please, just hire me back," she begged—Anna the proud, who never begged for anything.

He took her hand. He wanted to cover her with kisses, let her know that she was safe, let her know that he'd never let anyone hurt her again. "I'll keep you safe, and your family, too. I swear to you on my life."

"I just need a job." She licked her lips nervously— full pink lips that were made to be kissed. For a moment he couldn't stop looking at her mouth. Why hadn't he bedded her yet? Why hadn't he kissed her every hour, every moment? He tried to remember as she continued desperately, "I'll work from home so I can still take good care of the baby. And you'll be glad to have me back in your office, I promise. I'll make you so glad—"

"No," he said harshly, furious at how tempted he was to give in to her. Hell, he'd love to have her as his secretary again. His life was so much easier with Anna by his side. And it was hard for him to deny her anything when he wanted to kiss her so badly. But he couldn't be selfish. Not now. "I don't want you as my secretary. I want you as my wife."

"Nikos, please," she whispered, with those full pink lips. She crossed her arms over her chest, pushing her breasts upwards beneath her slim white shirt. "I need this so badly—"

So did he.

Taking her in his arms, he kissed her.

CHAPTER SEVEN

ANNA could not even try to stop him. His kiss was hot, demanding. She felt his fingers run down her neck and along her back, and her whole body seemed to relax like a sigh. For a brief moment she thought she could put all her cares and worries aside. She was safe in his arms. Maybe Nikos could protect her, care for her. Love her…

His tongue brushed against hers as he deepened the kiss, caressing her in an erotic dance that left her breathless. She leaned against him with a sigh.

"Anna," he whispered, so softly that the words were a mere breath against her skin. "You belong with me. Always."

He pressed her against the desk, kissing the vulnerable spot between her neck and shoulder until prickles of longing spread across her body. He ran his hands through her hair, causing bobby pins to scatter to the floor and her hair to tumble out of its chignon around her shoulders. She braced herself with an unsteady hand against his muscled shoulder. His fingers played with the waistband of her black pencil skirt, then moved beneath her fitted white shirt. A gasp escaped her as she felt his wide fingers splay lightly against the skin of her belly.

Without warning he lifted her up on the desk, crushing papers beneath her weight, cradling her to his body. He spread her legs to wrap them around him. Through his finely cut trousers, she could feel how badly he wanted her.

She wanted him too. But she was afraid. Afraid to trust too much, to give too much. What if she let herself depend on him and he crushed her?

She couldn't let herself give in to her desire. If she agreed to be his wife it would mean disaster. She couldn't give herself away to a man who didn't love her!

He drew away. "You're trembling."

Grasping at straws, she indicated the résumés, their laptops, the appointment calendars spread across his large mahogany desk. "We can't do this," she panted. "There's too much at stake—"

With an angry growl, he swept everything on the desk to the floor. Not even seeming to notice the crash of the laptops as they hit the carpet, he pushed her backward against the glossy wood of the desk. "Here. Now."

"Nikos—"

He leaned forward, pressing his body against hers. His face inches from hers, his dark eyes pierced hers as he looked into her own searchingly. "Tell me that you don't want this. Tell me you don't want *me*."

Licking her lips, she tried to speak the words. But the lies could not form themselves on her mouth when all she wanted to do was kiss him all over and feel his naked skin against her body.

She closed her eyes as she felt him slowly unbuttoning her shirt. He kissed her bare skin with each newly revealed inch until he finally pulled the shirt off her body. Without even knowing what she was doing, she whispered, "Please."

He stopped. "Please what?"

Please hurry.

Please make love to me now.

Please love me...

"Wait," she gasped. To her surprise, he released her, and, bereft of his touch, she opened her eyes.

He pushed himself up on one arm, looking down at her, and the expression on his face was one she'd never seen before. No, that wasn't true. She'd seen it once. The night they'd conceived Misha. Nikos Stavrakis, the ruthless billionaire, was watching her with a vulnerable light in his dark eyes. As if she alone had the power to hurt him. Or save him.

"What is it, *zoe mou?*" he asked softly.

"I'm afraid," she blurted out, then stopped, aghast.

"Of what?"

"I'm afraid you'll hurt me," she whispered.

A smile suddenly curved his lips, softening the hard angles of his handsome face as he gently brushed her cheek with his hand. "I would never hurt you, *agape mou.* Never."

And at that moment she believed him.

"I will be gentle. I swear to you on my life." With two easy movements he pulled off her skirt, murmuring with awe, "You are so beautiful."

She reached up for him, unbuttoning his crisp linen shirt. Unlike his easy removal of her clothes, her fingers felt clumsy. They trembled in excitement, until finally she gave up on the last button and ripped off the shirt in her impatience.

"That was my favorite shirt," he said, amused.

"Stupid of you to wear it today," she murmured.

Growling under his breath, he braced himself with his knees on the desk over her and slowly stroked down her full breasts, beneath the lacy fabric of her bra, until the only sound she could make was a moan.

He unhooked the front clasp of her bra and pulled the fabric off her body, tossing it to the floor. "Beautiful," he breathed again, cupping them in his hands, and she arched her back against the desk, straining to bring him closer to her. He lowered his head to taste her breasts. Then abruptly stopped.

Wondering why, she looked down and saw that a small trickle of milk had escaped her left breast. She felt a squirm of embarrassment, then defiance. She was a nursing mother. She wouldn't, couldn't, be ashamed of it. But still…

He raised a dark eyebrow at her, then lowered his head and slowly licked the other breast with his rough tongue. She sighed with pleasure. She gasped as he lowered his head between her legs.

He worked his tongue with agonizing slowness, spreading her wide to taste the very heart of her. The full thickness of his tongue seemed to touch every nerve-ending of her body, leaving her quivering and taut with longing.

Gripping his hair with her hands, she stared up at the ceiling, knowing she should make him stop, that she should pull away, but she couldn't. She was naked in his office, her thighs spread wide on his mahogany desk, and her boss—the playboy desired by women far more beautiful than she—was lapping her with his tongue until she thought she would explode.

And then she did. She heard a loud cry and realized it had come from her own mouth. For a few seconds afterward all she could do was breathe, and Nikos took her in his arms, holding her close as he whispered endearments. Anna realized that he wasn't even all the way naked. But he was all the way hard. She could feel that through his tailored pants, pressing against her. And yet he wasn't trying to make love to her.

Why not?

She started to stroke him through the fabric, but he caught her hands. His eyes, looking down at her, were vulnerable. "Marry me, Anna. Be my wife."

Yes.

Yes.

God, yes.

"I can't." It felt horrible to say. Ungenerous and so, so wrong. And it wasn't what she wanted. Especially when it made him abruptly pull away. "We can raise our son together, but I can't marry you, Nikos. It would never work."

"So you say." He pulled away from her and without even looking in her direction started to put on his shirt.

She sat up, still naked, feeling dizzy. "Don't you understand? We'd never be happy together."

"No, I don't understand. I see only a spoiled woman who is determined to toss away happiness with both hands."

"You don't love me—" she started, praying he would argue.

Instead, he cut her off with, "And you don't love me." His face, so warm and loving just moments before, now expressed icy contempt. "But we both love our son. I am trying to do what's best for him. I wish you would do the same."

"I am!" she said, stung.

"Right." He rapidly buttoned up his shirt. "What have I done to make you hate me, Anna? What did I do that was so horrible? What have I ever done except try to take care of all of us? One of us has to take responsibility for the family we've created. Especially since you obviously don't give a damn."

"Wait—that's not true—you know it's not true!"

His lip curled as he turned to go. "I'm going to go find Sinistyn and handle him once and for all. Before he talks his way into becoming Michael's stepfather. Because apparently you have a problem telling him no. Unlike me."

"I'm not trying to hurt you. I just don't want you to get involved."

"Too late."

"It's not your problem, it's mine. I should be the one to—"

"My God, you really don't trust me at all, do you?

No matter what I do or say, you won't accept my help. You'd rather fight me. You'd rather put both yourself and our son in danger." He stopped in the doorway. "I always admired you, Anna. A pity the good sense you have as a secretary is lacking in you as a woman."

His words struck her to the bone. His face was in shadow as he added quietly, "Look through the résumés, Anna. Find me a new secretary. When I come back, give me a name. I'm done fighting with you."

Nikos was grim as he rode in the back of his limo, poring through documents about the last-minute details of the Singapore land lease bid as his chauffeur drove him back to the casino.

He'd lost his temper.

He never lost his temper.

Damn it, Anna was really starting to get to him. He'd accused her of letting her emotions run her reason, but he had just done the same.

The way he'd shouted at her. It made him wince now. It had not gone according to plan. Yelling at her was no way to make her fall in love. Even he knew that.

He sighed, leaning his head against the darkened glass and staring out at the empty, barren landscape as the Nevada desert flew by. He'd felt so close. His soul had soared when he'd felt her tremble beneath his tongue. He'd felt sure that she would say yes to his proposal. Why else had he restrained himself, when he could think of nothing but having her in his bed? He'd said that he wanted to make love to her only as his wife, and that was still true.

He ground his teeth. Forget those stupid scruples. He only had twenty-four hours to close the deal. Next time he wouldn't hesitate. He wouldn't relent. He'd seduce her, and he'd get both his satisfaction and her agreement to his proposal. And before she had a chance to change her mind he'd take her straight to one of the all-night wedding chapels and get it all nailed down.

He glanced at the document still in his briefcase. His lawyers had already drawn up the standard prenuptial agreement: if the marriage should end, both parties would end up with what they'd started with. Leaving Anna virtually penniless.

He didn't intend for her to suffer. On the contrary, he meant for her to live in luxury. He'd even keep her snooty mother in Hermès handbags. Anything to make Anna happy. The prenup was for one reason only—to make sure that Anna would never have any incentive to walk away from their marriage.

He twisted his neck, cracking the joints to relieve the stress, and revised his tattered gameplan. Tonight was his last night to close the deal. After he'd finished with Sinistyn he'd go straight home, make love to Anna until she couldn't see straight, and then she'd sign the prenup. Then they'd go to the courthouse for a license and, from there, a drive-thru chapel.

He flexed his hands, trying to make himself relax. Anna was getting under his skin—probably because they were spending so much time together, blending home and work. It had been wonderful, in a way, having her back in the office. Best damn secretary he'd ever had. Together they were the perfect team. Unbeatable.

No. He pushed the thought away. He'd already made up his mind, and tonight it would be done. He'd get a new secretary, take Anna as his wife, and keep his home and work life separate—the way they were supposed to be. He'd enjoy Anna at night, see his son every day, and go back to putting in eighteen-hour days at the office. That was the life that made sense to him. That was a life he could control.

But Anna *had* to marry him. Without that everything else fell apart.

Rubbing his hand against his forehead, he sighed. It was time for him to play his last card. He had no choice. He was leaving for Singapore tomorrow, to meet with government officials and make sure Stavrakis Resorts' land lease bid was successful. The new casino resort would be an important asset in his son's fortune.

But first he had to close the deal with Anna.

He would tell her he loved her.

He'd never said the words before—to anyone. And even tonight it would be a lie. He would lie to make her capitulate, to make her love him in return. He'd told himself that he'd never say those three words to anyone, but he'd give up that tiny slice of honor now. He'd do far more than that to protect his family.

He'd tell her he loved her, and make her believe it. He had to convince her he meant it. Convince her he'd make a good husband. Convince her he was worthy of her love, even if it all was a lie…

He had a sudden memory of Anna in his bed, naked, with tousled hair and a sweetly seductive smile, looking up at him with honest, trusting eyes.

He shook the disturbing image away. As his chauffeur pulled up to the private garage on the third level parking deck of L'Hermitage, he focused instead on his meeting with Victor Sinistyn, whom he'd called on the drive into town.

He couldn't blame the man for wanting Anna for himself. Nikos ground his teeth as he strode into his private elevator. Any man would want Anna. But Sinistyn had gone too far, trying to force her into a marriage against her will. Trying to *buy* her through trickery and putting pressure on her family.

Images of Anna went through his mind: laughing in the pool last week, splashing with their child, smiling up at Nikos in the bright sunlight. She was so beautiful, so vibrant, so warm and alive. How *dare* Sinistyn try to imprison her? How dare he try to seize by manipulation and force something he had no right to call his own?

"It's time you picked on someone your own size," Nikos muttered under his breath as he entered his private office.

"What was that, sir?" Margaret, the senior administrative assistant for the casino, was filling in on some rudimentary duties as his executive secretary. She temporarily sat in Anna's old desk outside his office.

"Please let me know when Victor Sinistyn arrives."

Closing the door behind him, he went to the outside windows and stared down at Las Vegas Boulevard, watching the hectic traffic below. He went to the crystal decanter and started to pour himself a small bourbon, then stopped.

Was it possible that he was doing the same thing as Sinistyn? Trying to possess Anna when he had no right?

No, he told himself fiercely. It wasn't the same at all. Sinistyn was trying to force Anna to marry him to satisfy his own selfish lust. Nikos just wanted to protect his family. To protect his son.

But still, the voice of conscience, rusty from disuse, whispered in his mind, *you're going to make her fall in love with you on false pretenses, to bind her to you forever. Isn't that just as bad?*

He tried to shake the thought out of his mind, but it wouldn't go away. He paced back and forth through his office, trying to concentrate on Sinistyn, the Singapore deal—anything but his plans for Anna. In the end he gave up, and pummeled the boxing bag in the corner of his office with his bare hands to clear his mind. The pain helped him forget. Helped him focus.

There was blood on two knuckles when he went over to the wall of one-sided windows that overlooked the main casino floor. He glanced down, impatiently looking at his watch. Sinistyn was two minutes late.

Then his eyes sharpened.

Sinistyn wasn't late. He was already in the casino downstairs, beneath the high crystal chandeliers, in between the gilded nineteenth-century columns and wealthy, attractive gamblers at the roulette tables and slot machines.

He wasn't alone, either. He'd brought two hulking bodyguards from his club. But he wasn't talking to them.

He was talking to Anna.

Anna. Still wearing the slim white shirt and black skirt, but sexier than ever, with her long, long legs and glossy black pumps. Her dark hair, which he'd mussed so thoroughly nearly making love to her on his desk, cascaded down her shoulders. Her lips were full, pink and bruised, as if she'd just come from bed.

She was too enticing—innocence and sin wrapped up into one luscious package.

Nikos cursed under his breath. She'd defied his direct orders and come down here to intercept Sinistyn. He clenched his jaw. From this distance he couldn't read the expressions on their faces. What was she saying to him? What was he saying to her? His hands clenched into fists as he strode out of his office to the elevator.

When he reached the casino floor he signaled Cooper, his head of security, to follow with two bodyguards. Trailing bodyguards in his wake, he stalked through the noise of slot machines and gamblers toward Anna and Sinistyn, barely able to keep his fury in check.

Why couldn't she trust him to handle things? Not even once? Why did she always have to make everything *so damned hard*?

"Sinistyn," he said coldly, grabbing the man's

shoulder. "Let's go upstairs to talk." He gave Anna a look. "Leave."

"I'm staying," she said, raising her chin.

He heard Sinistyn snicker under his breath. Nikos ground his teeth. "Let me handle this."

"This isn't your fight. It's mine." To Nikos's shock, she turned to Victor Sinistyn and put her hand on his hairy arm, looking deep and soulfully into his eyes. "Victor, I'm sorry this has gone so far. It's my fault."

"About time you came to your senses, *loobemaya*. I've waited long enough for you to be my wife." Looking up from her cleavage with a triumphant half-smile, he locked eyes with Nikos. "About time you chose the better man."

Nikos felt a strange lurch in his chest. A sick feeling spread through his body. She'd chosen Sinistyn over him? She trusted that man over him?

"No." Anna was shaking her head at Sinistyn. "That's what I'm trying to tell you. I'm sorry, but I don't love you, Victor. I never have. I should have made it clear from the first time you flirted with me, ten years ago. I will never be with you. No matter how much money you loan my parents. Never."

The smug expression disappeared from Sinistyn's face. He looked dangerous and hard. "You don't know what you're saying."

"You bought the palace for nothing. I'll pay you back the money we owe. But I don't want you."

His eyes became hooded, his face flushed with anger. "At the club last week you made me think differently."

She took a deep breath and looked him straight in the eye. "I was going to ask for your help to get custody of my son. It was wrong of me. But then you were wrong to loan my parents millions of dollars at a thirty-five percent interest rate while claiming to be our friend."

"Your father promised that you would be mine. When we were in business together he said he'd convince you—"

"He tried, but I refused. We've known each other for a long time, Victor. It is time for us to be honest. I will never be your wife, but I will pay back every dime we owe you. Can we at least part as friends?"

She held out her hand.

But Victor's expression was hard as he looked from her outstretched hand to her face. He grabbed her arm roughly, causing her to cry out.

"I waited for you," he said softly. "I've tried to be nice. But it seems there's only one language you'll understand. You're mine, Anna. Mine."

He drew back a fist. Sucking in her breath, she winced in anticipation.

Quick as a flash, Nikos stepped between them, grabbing the other man's hand. He knocked him off balance with a hard right hook and shoved him to the ground.

"Don't touch her," Nikos shouted. "Not now. Not ever."

His body was crying out for the man's blood. He wanted to bash Victor Sinistyn into a pulp for threatening her. He wanted to kill the man for trying to hurt her.

Then he heard Anna's soft moan.

Nikos realized that his own bodyguards were barely keeping Sinistyn's men in check, and that at any moment a full brawl would break out in his own casino. They were already being watched by gamblers, gawkers and slack-jawed tourists, a couple of whom were holding cameras in anticipation of the coming action.

Breathing hard, Nikos jerked away from Sinistyn. "Get him out of here," he ordered Cooper. Cooper nodded, and with a single gesture a phalanx of security guards appeared.

"Follow me, gentlemen," Cooper said, holding out his arm in an ironic gesture.

One of Sinistyn's bodyguards tried to help his boss to his feet, but the Russian jerked his arm away and rose slowly on his own.

"You'll regret this, Stavrakis," Sinistyn said, and then his eyes shifted to Anna. "You'll both regret this."

He stormed out, followed closely by his shamefaced bodyguards.

"I'll make sure he doesn't get back in," Cooper said quietly. "And post extra guards on the night watch." He said loudly to the crowd, "Show's over, folks. The waitresses will be out to make sure everyone's getting their drinks."

Nikos felt Anna in his arms as she threw herself against his chest. "Oh, Nikos, I'm so sorry. It's all my fault."

At her touch, he slowly came back to himself. He looked down at her, stroking her hair.

"Everything you said was right," she said tearfully.

"Everything. I should have trusted you. I've been a fool. A selfish, cowardly fool." She pressed her face against his shirt with a sob, then looked up at him, tears streaming down her pale cheeks. "I ran away when you were only trying to protect us. Can you ever forgive me?"

Nikos had been right about Victor.

Anna's stomach hurt. She'd known Victor was bad, but she'd never thought he'd actually want to hurt her. Natalie had also tried to tell her, but she wouldn't listen.

Nikos had been right about everything. Maybe he'd been bossy and controlling, but at least his motives had been good. Strong and loyal and true, he'd put their new little family first in his life. Why hadn't she done the same? Why hadn't she been brave enough to stay and fight, rather than believe the worst of him?

"Forgive me," she said again.

His dark eyes were unreadable as he softly touched her lips with his finger. "There is nothing to forgive."

She was suddenly aware of the curious stares of onlookers and the noise of the slot machines. "Before you leave for Asia, I need to talk to you."

"Let's go upstairs." He hugged her close to his body, guiding her gently toward the private elevator. His body felt warm against hers. She wrapped her hand around his muscular waist, enveloped in the scent of him—clean, but with a hint of something dangerous, as searing as the desert sun.

She knew the risk of reaching for the sun. Its heat and fire could consume her.

But she was suddenly so tired of feeling frozen inside.

Nikos had made it clear that he was done fighting with her. She'd been praying that she would have changed his mind by now, that she'd have proved she could both be a good mother and a good employee. But it was too late. He didn't want her as his secretary. He wanted her to fulfill their deal.

She'd blown it.

Once they were upstairs he'd demand the name of his new secretary. She'd give it to him, and tomorrow he would fly off for Singapore. There would be nothing left for her to do but pack for a new life in New York.

A new life that, for all its freedoms, would be missing one thing she wanted desperately. The man she loved.

She loved him. There. She'd admitted it—if only to herself. But he didn't want to hire her, and without his love she didn't want to marry him. There was nothing left to say.

Except that if their relationship had to end she wanted one last night to remember. One night to laugh with him again. To be daring. To be bold. One night where she allowed herself to love him with her whole heart.

One night to prove how much she trusted him.

But, as much as she knew he wanted her, he'd already refused her too many times, holding out for marriage. She licked her lips, glancing at him from beneath her lashes. Before he left, could she make him change his mind—just for one night?

She'd never seduced a man in her life, but maybe it was time to try.

Marveling at her own boldness as she crossed the casino floor with his arm around her, she ran her fingers surreptitiously along his waistband, stroking his flat belly through his shirt. "You changed your shirt."

She heard his intake of breath, but his voice was even as he replied, "You ripped up the last one."

"Sorry." She rubbed her breast against his side as they walked. She heard a slight growl from his throat.

"What are you doing?"

"What do you mean?" she asked innocently.

He picked up his pace toward the elevator, and the moment the doors were closed behind them he was on her. Pressing her against the cool metal wall, he kissed her savagely, running his hands up and down her body.

"God, you drive me crazy," he whispered against her skin. "I want you, Anna. It's killing me."

"Good." She reached for his shirt and saw his expression as she untucked the fabric and ran her hands underneath, exploring his flat belly and the muscular chest covered with dark hair. "This time you're not going to refuse me," she said, using a tone she'd heard him use many times—the tone no one could refuse. She unbuttoned his shirt, her fingers somehow moving deftly, as if she'd been seducing men all her life. "You're not going to make me wait. You're not going to demand that I marry you."

"Anna." His breathing was coming harder. "We both know—"

"Later." She already knew what he was going to say, and she didn't want to hear a word of it. She didn't want to think about the résumés in her purse, or the fact that Nikos had finally decided to let her go. Tomorrow she'd face those cold, hard facts. But tonight she'd stop time. She'd have one perfect night with him that could be crystallized in her memory forever—something to remember during all the cold and lonely nights.

Tonight she would give herself to him completely.

I love you, Nikos. I love you.

"Did you say something?" he murmured.

Oh, my God, had she whispered those words aloud? She had to distract him.

"I said *no talking*." She reached for his waist. Unbuckling his belt, she pulled it out of the loops and tossed it to the floor of the elevator. She slowly stroked his bare belly beneath his shirt, swaying her body against his.

With a taunting smile, she undid the top button of his pants.

He gave an audible gasp and grabbed her wrists, yanking them tight above her head. "Is this what you want?" he choked out. "Hard and fast? Here in the elevator?"

She struggled against the shackles of his hands, wanting to touch him, to feel his naked skin against her own. Her whole body ached for him.

The elevator dinged as it reached their floor, and the doors slid open. She felt drunk, drugged with desire, as with a throaty growl Nikos picked her up, carrying her roughly into the penthouse.

Against a backdrop of two-story-high windows, the

only color was a minimalist red sofa against white walls and white carpet. He took her swiftly into his enormous bedroom. He pressed a button on the wall and the room suddenly glowed with firelight. She'd wondered what this room would be like. It was spartan, empty, and ghostly white. The floor was white tile, covered by a white fur rug in front of a white adobe fireplace. Surrounded by oceans of unused space, the king-sized bed sat, pristine and untouched, in the center of the room.

Nikos started to kiss her again, and she closed her eyes. She forgot where she was, forgot everything. He lowered her gently to the enormous mattress, caressing her long hair. He stroked her cheek, down her neck, then placed his hand softly between her breasts, over her heart.

"Last chance to leave," he growled.

Deliberately, she leaned back against his bed.

Unblinking as a wolf, he stared at her. Her eyes devoured his bare chest. Dark hair covered his torso, tightening to a vertical line that disappeared beneath the waistband of his exquisitely tailored pants.

His clothes were elegant and fine. The uniform of a wealthy, civilized man. But his body was something else, something more. As he discarded his clothes, tossing them on the white tile floor, he revealed the savage warrior beneath.

He stood in front of her, naked and unselfconscious. His muscles were hard, wide. She saw the old scars, almost faded, brought into stark relief by new white lines across his ribs and collarbone. She saw how much he wanted her. Most of all she saw his dark eyes, hungry with need. She sat up, reaching for him, holding out her arms.

He was on her in an instant, pressing her back roughly against the luxuriant softness of the bed.

"*Agape mou,*" he whispered. "I have waited so long. Wanted you for so long…"

Reaching his broad hands beneath her back, he unzipped her skirt. He pulled his shirt over her head and tossed them both to the floor. The stroke of the fabric, the sheen of his breath, sent prickles of longing up and down her skin. As he kissed slowly down her body, between her breasts and down her belly, it was all she could do not to blurt out the three forbidden words.

Kissing her, he pushed her back against the soft goosedown comforter, spreading his hands wide as he caressed her body, making her shiver as he ran his fingers over her white panties and bra.

He covered her with his naked body, pressing her into the soft folds of the thick comforter. She felt as if she was drowning. She clutched at him like a life preserver, gasping as he unhooked her bra and freed her breasts. He slowly moved his body up against hers, rubbing his chest against her, pressing his naked hardness between her legs as he sucked on her neck, her shoulder, her earlobes. Holding her tightly, he ran his tongue around the tender edge of her ear, slowly moving inward until he made her gasp as he penetrated the center with his tongue. She turned her face to him, grabbing the back of his head as she kissed him hungrily.

Then she pulled away, looking into his eyes.

She had to say the words. She couldn't keep them inside anymore.

"Nikos, I love you."

CHAPTER EIGHT

NIKOS froze. "What?"

"I love you." Anna's face looked bare, vulnerable, as she repeated the words.

Nikos had tried for the last hour to speak those same three words—the simple lie that would close the deal and give him the upper hand. But he'd been unable to force the words out of his mouth. He hadn't wanted to say them, hadn't wanted to lie to her. He'd let himself hope that making love to her would be enough.

Tsou. No. It was now or never. He had to act now, or it was all over.

He pictured his son with a man like Sinistyn as his stepfather. He imagined Anna in another man's arms, and his lips pressed into a line. To protect his family he'd do anything, say anything, sacrifice anything.

Even his honor.

Watching his face with a troubled expression, Anna rushed to say, "I know you don't love me back, and it's okay—"

"I love you, too." He spoke the words quickly, spitting them out as if they were a live grenade in his mouth.

"You love me?" Anna stared at him in amazement, as if she couldn't believe what she'd heard.

"Yes." His voice was low, strained.

Her whole face started to light up from within, like a thousand Christmas candles glowing at once. "You love me?" she repeated in a whisper, her eyes filling with tears. If he'd truly loved her, the joy on her face would have been enough to keep him warm through a thousand cold, dark winters. "I never expected—I never dreamed—Oh, Nikos…"

She kissed him then with a passion so pure and sweet it was unlike anything he'd ever known. He returned her kiss with fervor, desperate to forget the lie he'd told, to wipe his sin clean through the fire of his longing for her. He wanted her. He wanted every part of her. Her beauty and innocence and goodness. He kissed her back with all the hard, brutal honesty in his soul.

He ran his hands down the length of her soft skin, kissing her lips, her breasts, sucking the tips of her fingers as she reached for him, trying to pull him closer. The way she moved, the sway and tremble of her body beneath him, brought him perilously close to exploding. Only the thin barrier of fabric kept him from seizing her hips and plunging himself into her. The image had barely crossed his mind before he kissed down her belly, running his hands beneath the fabric, gently nudging her panties down as his kisses went lower. He pulled the cotton down with his teeth even as he ran his fingers between her splayed legs, lightly tracing upwards from the sensitive area behind her knees to her inner thighs. He reached his hands beneath her panties and pulled them down. His tongue descended on her, spreading and licking her wide. As he ran his tongue over her hot nub, swirling in a circular motion, she writhed and moaned beneath him.

"No—" she gasped, trying to push him away. "I want you inside me—"

But he was merciless. Instead of stopping, he reached a thick finger inside her, then another finger. He pushed into her as his tongue licked and lapped her. She arched violently, her body snapping back against the bed, and he felt her shake and tremble as she came.

Feeling like he was going to explode, he lifted up on his arms and positioned himself between her legs. He found her wet core, pressing right into her, then hesitated, panting from the effort of restraint. He didn't want to hurt her. He would have to go slowly…

But Anna, more merciful than he, took things into her own hands. As he gritted his teeth, aching as he pushed himself slowly inside her, she reached behind him and yanked his naked buttocks towards her, forcing him through the tight sheath, impaling her. He heard her gasp, and he tried to pull back, but the pleasure of being buried deep inside her after all the months of longing was too much. He moaned her name softly, moving inside her, and took her in his arms, kissing her.

He'd never known it could be like this.

* * *

It hurt when he pushed into her. Had he always been this big?

Then he kissed her. His tongue twined around hers, caressing her deeply, and as her body relaxed the pleasure returned, built, intensified.

He loves me, she thought in amazement. Her eyes fluttered open and she saw the expression on his face as he was kissing her. It was worshipful. Devout. Intent. *He loves me.*

Her body relaxed. She didn't have to leave him, ever. Her heart was flooded with joy such as she'd never known before. He'd never said *I love you* before.

With those three words her whole world had changed.

Somehow everything would work out. Why not? What problem was insurmountable, what miracles were impossible, when Nikos loved her?

Running his hands along her breasts, he slowly pushed into her again. Her nerves grew taut. She wanted him, wanted more. She lifted her hips to meet his thrust, holding on to his shoulders. But the bed was far too soft, swallowing her into the comforter under his weight.

With a growl of frustration he lifted her up from the bed, careful not to pull out as he wrapped her naked body around him. In five long steps he crossed the firelit room to the nearest wall—the thick windows that overlooked the Las Vegas Strip, twenty floors below. Thick, unbreakable windows that she herself had discussed with the architects—but she'd never dreamed she would put them to use like this.

Anna moaned as he pressed her naked body against

the windows. She glanced down at his tanned skin, at the ripple of his hard muscles in the flickering firelight. She tightened her legs around his rock-hard buttocks as he pushed into her. A groan came from his lips as he thrust into her again and again, causing her full breasts to move with each force of his thrust. Leaning forward, he bit her neck as the pleasure began to spiral within her, even deeper and harder than she'd felt before. Her whole body began to shake, so tense that she could hardly breathe for want of him. She felt him explode inside her with a shout, and she screamed, rocked hard against the windows behind her, as she was devoured by the most intense pleasure she'd ever known.

She fell forward onto him, weak and spent. He lifted her in his arms and lowered her to the white bearskin rug in front of the fire. Murmuring her name tenderly, kissing her face, he held her close.

It took Anna several minutes to open her eyes, but when she did Nikos was looking down at her. His dark eyes were fierce, guarded.

"Anna—" he said, then stopped.

She licked her lips uncertainly. Was he already thinking that he'd made a mistake telling her he loved her? Or maybe she'd imagined the whole thing? Suddenly she felt afraid. For a long moment she heard only the low roar of the fire.

He reached down to caress her cheek. "I don't want to be like Sinistyn. Answer me this one last time, and I promise you I will never ask again." He took a deep breath. "Will you marry me?"

A rush of relief and joy went through her.

"Yes," she said.

He visibly exhaled. "Tonight? Right now?"

She snickered, playfully tugging on his ear. "We'll have to get a license, won't we? The courthouse closed hours ago."

"I'll call the judge at home—"

"No. Let's do this right. Please."

"Tomorrow, then?" he growled. "First thing in the morning?"

"All right," she said, kissing his cheek and smiling.

"You're really going to marry me?"

"Yes!"

"Say it again," he ordered, holding her close.

She laughed out of pure happiness. "Nikos, I'll marry you."

As Nikos held Anna in his arms through the long, interminable night, he stared up at the moonlight creeping slowly across the ceiling above the wide bed. He held her close, listening to her sighs of sleep against his bare shoulder. She was so sweet. So trusting.

And he'd deceived her.

I did what I had to do, he told himself fiercely. Anna would be his forever. Michael would have a permanent family. He'd saved his family. He'd matched his wits against hers, laying siege against her heart until it fell, like a golden city overrun by a savage army.

But he'd never thought winning would feel like this.

He'd lied to her. Now, even holding her in his arms,

so warm and soft against him, he felt cold. He stared down at her lovely face in the shadows and moonlight. She was smiling in her sleep, pressing her body against his. She was radiating warmth and contentment. She believed that he finally loved her. She believed in happy endings—even for a man like him.

His whole body was racked with tension. But even as he tried to justify what he'd done the thought that she would learn soon enough about his lie pounded through him. She wouldn't be satisfied with an unlimited bank account in lieu of his love. She would demand things of him—emotion, energy, vulnerability—that he simply couldn't give. Not even if he tried. He just wasn't made that way.

And as soon as she found out how she'd been deceived, her joy would be snuffed out like a candle. It would cause the bright new light in her to go out, perhaps forever.

Shortly before dawn he heard snuffling moans from the next room, where Mrs. Burbridge had brought their baby to spend the night. At their son's cries, Anna stirred in his arms.

She gently pushed out of his embrace and crept into the baby's room to nurse, before returning back into his bed.

"Nikos?" Anna whispered.

He kept his breathing even, feigning sleep.

"Thank you," she said, so quietly it was barely audible. "I have the home I dreamed of, the family I dreamed of. I don't know what I did to deserve this. Thank you for loving me."

God, this was intolerable. He turned on his side, pulling away from her, every nerve taut. As soon as he was sure she was really asleep, he sat up in bed. Feeling bone-weary, he raked his hands through his hair and rose slowly from the bed.

Glancing at Anna, slumbering peacefully beneath the white goosedown comforter, he came to a decision. He looked at the clock. It was almost six. He'd intended to have her sign the prenuptial agreement as soon as she woke, then drive straight to the courthouse for a license. He'd planned for them to be married at a drive-thru chapel before breakfast.

But, no matter how pure his motives, now that he held her fate in the palm of his hands he just couldn't do it. He couldn't take her honesty and trust and love and use them as weapons against her. He couldn't break her heart and destroy her life, no matter how good his motives might be.

Anna Rostoff deserved a man who could love her with his whole heart.

If he wasn't that man, he had to let her go.

A fine time to grow a conscience, Nikos thought bleakly. Apparently he did have one last bit of honor left.

He gave Anna one final, lingering glance. Her dark hair was sprawled across his pillow, her creamy skin like ivory against the white thousand-count sheets. Her cheeks still glowed pink, a remnant of their lovemaking, and her lips curved into a soft smile as she sighed in her sleep.

It was an image he knew he'd never see again.

Anna woke in a flood of early-morning light with one bright thought: today was her wedding day!

She stretched her limbs against the luxurious sheets with a contented yawn. Her body felt sore. A good kind of sore. She smiled to herself, almost blushing as she remembered everything Nikos had done to her last night. She'd woken up twice for the baby, but, as worn out as she'd been from their lovemaking, with Nikos's hard body curled protectively around hers she'd still had an amazing night's sleep.

She glanced over to the wall of windows, revealing the wide blue Nevada sky from the twentieth-floor penthouse. She'd never felt happy like this before. Safe. Optimistic. Secure. For the first time in her whole life she not only had a home, she had someone who would actually watch over and protect her, instead of just looking out for their own interests. And she had someone she could protect and love in return not because she had to, but because she wanted to.

She and Nikos would be partners, in work as in life. Together they'd be as unbreakable as tempered steel.

It was an exquisitely heady feeling. She wanted to do cartwheels across the penthouse.

She wanted to kiss Nikos *right now*.

Where was he? In the kitchen, making her breakfast? Humming to herself, she rose from the bed and threw on a satin robe, barely stopping long enough to loosely tie the belt to cover her naked body. She paused briefly outside the door of the second bedroom, where Misha was sleeping. She heard only blessed silence.

She smiled to herself. With any luck she and Nikos

would have time for more than a kiss before their child woke up demanding breakfast.

She went down the hall and found the kitchen, but it was empty. The immaculate white counters looked as if they'd never even been touched. Nikos was probably already working in his office. Wouldn't he be surprised and happy if she made him coffee, eggs and toast?

Looking in the bare cupboards and refrigerator, she made a face. Even she couldn't manage to manufacture breakfast out of sugar cubes, Greek olives and ice. She turned away when she heard voices down the hall. She followed the sound, stopping outside the door at the other end of the hall.

Muffled through the door, she heard a man's voice say, "Sir, in my opinion you're making an enormous mistake. As your attorney, I must advise—"

"Since I'm paying you five hundred dollars an hour, I won't waste more time discussing it. I've heard your complaints. Thank you for your assistance. There's the door."

Anna's ear was pressed against the wood; she jumped as the door was flung open and an older man in a dark gray suit came through it.

He gave her a sharp glance, then a scowl. "Congratulations, miss." He put on his hat and stomped out of the apartment with his briefcase.

"Anna. You're awake," Nikos said. "Come in."

His face was dark, half hidden in the shadows of morning where he sat behind a black lacquer desk. The furniture here was as sleek and soulless as everything else in this penthouse. Anna suddenly felt uneasy.

"I thought you were going to wake me up," she said. "Early-morning wedding and all that." She glanced behind her. "Why was your lawyer here? Oh. He brought the prenup?"

His eyes flicked at her in surprise. "You knew I wanted you to sign a prenuptial agreement?"

"I assumed you would. I mean, of course you'd want me to sign one. You're a wealthy man," she said lamely, even as disappointment surged through her. He didn't trust her. He honestly thought she cared about his money, that she'd try to take it. He thought they were at risk of getting a divorce. It cast a pall over her happiness.

Then she realized what he'd said. "Wait a minute. You *wanted* for me to sign a prenup? But not any more?"

"No," he said quietly. "Not any more."

She blinked as the joy came back through her. He'd realized he could trust her!

"Nikos," she breathed. She crossed the room in five steps and, pulling back his chair, climbed in his lap and threw her arms around him. "You won't regret it," she murmured against the warm skin of his neck. "I'll never let you down. I'll be true to you until the day I die. We're going to be so happy…"

She kissed him then, a long, lingering kiss that held her whole heart in every breath.

"Stop, Anna. Just stop." Pushing her off his lap, he stood up, rubbing his temples. His whole body was tense. He didn't seem like a man who was about to get married. He seemed miserable. And furious. Like a wounded lion with a thorn in his paw. He seemed both hurt and dangerous.

"What is it?" she asked warily. "What's wrong?"

He picked up a file from his desk and held it out to her without a word, careful not to let their hands touch. Pulling the papers out of the file, she looked down at the first page and her knees felt weak.

She looked up at him slowly, her mouth dry. "I don't…I don't understand."

"There's nothing to understand. I'm giving you joint custody. You can live wherever you like, and I'll provide you with a generous allowance. Enough to clear your family's debt. Enough to support your mother and sister. My brownstone in the Upper East Side will be transferred to your name. My son will have every support, the best schools, vacations abroad—whatever you think best. All I ask is that I have visitation at will, as well as some arrangement to be made for holidays."

Her head was spinning. "But I don't need custody papers. Once we're married we—"

He was shaking his head grimly. "That was a fairytale, Anna, nothing more. I wanted you in my bed, that's all."

"No." She frowned at him, feeling like she'd fallen into some strange nightmare. "You could have had me in your bed long ago. You were the one who insisted we wait. You've done everything under the sun to convince me to marry you. Why would you change your mind now? It doesn't make sense."

He gave her a careless smile. "I guess I'm just not marriage material."

"But you are!" she gasped. "I know you are. You've changed over the last weeks. You've become the husband I've always wanted, the father I dreamed of for Misha. Kind, brave, strong." She closed her eyes, a thousand images going through her of all the time they'd spent together over the last weeks. Working together. Laughing. Nikos playing with their child. "All the time we've spent together—"

"It was a trick, Anna. God, don't you get it? It was all an act. I wanted you. I would have pretended anything to win you. It was pride, I suppose. I couldn't stand the thought of you leaving me. But now—" he shrugged. "The charade's already growing old. I don't want the burden of a wife or the full-time care of a child. I want my freedom."

"It's not true! You're lying!"

He grabbed her wrist, searing her with his hot dark gaze. "You know me," he said cruelly. "You know how I am. So many beautiful women, so little time. Did you really think I could ever settle down with one woman? With you?"

She felt like she'd just gotten punched. She looked up into his face as tears filled her eyes. "Why are you saying this?"

For an instant something like regret and pain washed over his handsome face. "It's better for you to be free," he said finally. "Forget about me, Anna. You deserve a man who will truly love you."

"But *you* love me. You said so," she whispered.

He shook his head, and now his eyes were only cold. "I lied. I don't love anyone. I don't know how."

At those words, all the hope she'd been holding in her chest disappeared.

Nikos didn't love her. He'd chased her out of pride, out of his determination to possess her, to beat his rival. But now that she'd given him her heart he was already bored with her.

For the first time she believed him, and she felt sick. She turned away.

"Fine." She was relieved that her voice didn't tremble. She tried to remember the plan she'd once had—the plan that had sounded so wonderful before she'd fallen back in love with Nikos. "I guess I'll…I'll go back to New York and get a job."

"No." His voice was dark, inexorable. "I told you. You'll never need to work again."

She looked up at him, pressing her fingernails into her palms to fight back tears. She had her pride too— too much pride to ever cry in front of him again.

"I won't take a penny from a man who doesn't love me. I'm going to find a job. Whether you give me a recommendation or not."

He blinked at her, then turned away, clenching his jaw. "I didn't want it to end like this."

"How did you expect it to end?"

He didn't answer the question. His dark eyes looked haunted as he gazed down at her. "You're right. If you truly want to work, I can't stop you. I have no right to stop you," he said in a low voice. "All I can do is ask that you make the decision carefully. And I know you will. I see now that you'll always look out for Misha. I just have one favor to ask. When you marry again, choose well. Choose carefully for our son."

"I thought I had," she said softly. Her feelings were rushing through her, almost uncontrollable. He'd finally agreed that she could work, but even that didn't matter anymore. She wanted to wrap her arms around him, to weep, to beg him not to leave her.

But she was the great-granddaughter of a princess. She was Misha's mother and she had to be strong. Anna clung to her dignity and pride. They were all she had left.

Reaching into her purse, she quietly handed him two pieces of paper. "Here."

"What are these?" he said, sounding shaken.

"The two best résumés for an executive secretary. I lied when I said they weren't any good because I hoped you'd hire me instead. But now that I'm leaving I don't want the company to suffer. I care too much about the company. I care too much about you. I love you."

"Anna—"

She stepped away from him, looking into his eyes. "Goodbye, Nikos. Good luck."

She turned to go, still praying he'd stop her.

He didn't.

Going into the next room, she found the overnight bag Mrs. Burbridge had packed for her the previous night and put on a T-shirt and jeans. She carefully placed the custody agreement into her old diaper bag. She fed and changed Misha and cuddled him close.

Taking a deep breath, she glanced down the hall, hoping against hope that Nikos would appear, put his strong arms around her, and tell her this had all been a horrible mistake.

But Nikos's office door remained closed.

He didn't even care enough to say goodbye. He was probably already phoning the employment agency about the résumés. Or maybe he was calling some sexy showgirl to ask for a date.

Apparently she was easy to replace. In every way.

Straightening, she held on to the frayed edges of her dignity and walked out of the penthouse where, just an hour ago, she'd thought she found love and security at last. She wouldn't let herself cry. Not in his casino, where his men and his security cameras were everywhere.

She managed to hold back her sobs until she reached the sidewalk on Las Vegas Boulevard. Where to now? There was a taxi stand at the hotel across the street. She could barely see through her tears as she stepped off the curb. Just in time she saw the van barreling toward her in the sparse early-morning traffic. She jumped back on the sidewalk in a cold sweat, frightened at how close she'd come to walking into traffic with her son.

"Just who I was looking for," a cold voice said. She looked up with a gasp to see Victor sitting inside the van's open door with several of his men. "What? No snappy comeback? Not so brave when you're alone, are you? Grab the kid," he ordered.

Anna started to fight and scream, trying to run away, but it was hopeless. When Misha was ripped from her arms she immediately surrendered. Ten seconds later she was tied up in the back of the van, on her way to hell. Victor faced her with cold eyes and an oily smile.

"You have a choice to make, *loobemaya*. What happens next is up to you."

Nikos had a sick feeling in his gut.

Pacing around his L'Hermitage penthouse, he poured himself a bourbon, then put it down untasted. He went to his home office, started to check his email, then closed the laptop without reading a single message. He finally went to the window overlooking Las Vegas. Twenty floors above the city, he had a clear view. He could see the wide desert beyond the city to the far mountains. It seemed to stretch forever. The emptiness was everywhere.

Especially here.

I did the right thing letting her go, he told himself. But the sick feeling only got worse. His knees felt weak, as if he'd just run twenty miles without stopping, or gone twenty rounds with a heavyweight champ; he sank into the sleek red-upholstered chair by the edge of the window. He put his head in his hands.

It was the silence that was killing him.

The absolute silence of his beautifully decorated apartment. No baby laughter. No lullabies from Anna. No voices at all. Just dead silence.

He could call one of his trusted employees, like Cooper. He could call acquaintances from the club. He could call any of a dozen women he'd dated. They would be here in less than ten minutes to fill his home with noise.

But he didn't want them.

He wanted his family.

He wanted *her*. His secretary. His lover. His friend.

"*I had to give her up*," he repeated to himself, raking his hand through his hair. I didn't love her.

"Are you sure about that, sir?" a Scottish voice said from behind him.

Nikos jumped when he realized he'd spoken his last words aloud. Mrs. Burbridge was standing in the doorway, her hands folded in front of her. A sharp reply rose to his lips, but her plump face looked so gentle and understanding he bit back the words. Instead, he muttered, "Of course I'm sure."

"You told me to pick up the baby early this morning, as you'd be going to a wedding, but I've arrived to find an open door, no wee babe, and no bride. Am I to understand the wedding's off?"

"They're both gone," he said wearily. He went to his desk, sat down and opened his checkbook. "Your job here is done, Mrs. Burbridge. I'm sorry to bring you so far for just a few weeks. I'll compensate you—"

She reached over and shut the checkbook with a bang. "Where are they, sir? Anna and your child?"

"I let them go," he said, resting his head in his hands. "My son deserved a mother."

"But the bairn was happy enough. So was his mother, I thought. Why send them away?"

"Because Anna deserves better," he exploded. "She deserves a man who can love her. She's been through enough. From her family. From me. I just want her to be happy."

"And you? You don't look terribly happy."

He gave a bitter laugh. "I'll get by. But Anna..." He rubbed the back of his head wearily. "I couldn't let her down. She loved me. Marrying me would have ruined her life."

"Her happiness means more to you than your own?"

"She's the mother of my son. The best damn partner I ever had at work. My friend. My lover. Of course I want her to be happy. It's all I want."

The Scotswoman raised her head and looked at him. Her eyes were kind, but sad. "Sir, what do you think love *is*?"

For a second he just stared at her. Then his heart started to pound in his chest.

"Oh, my God," he whispered.

Was it possible that she was right? That he *loved* Anna?

He didn't just want her in his bed, that was true. He didn't just enjoy her company, appreciate her skills as a mother or respect her perfect secretarial work.

He wanted her face to be the first he woke up to and the last he saw before he slept.

He wanted to see her face light up when she had a business idea, or when she was splashing around in the pool with their son.

He wanted her to be happy. To work as his secretary if that was what it took to make her glow from the inside out. Her happiness was everything.

That was love?

Oh, my God. *He loved her*. He didn't deserve her, but what if he could spend the rest of his life striving to make her happy?

Because without Anna he now realized that his life was empty. His fortune, his business empire—meant nothing. Without her this penthouse was no better than his childhood tenement, and his life was just as lonely and hungry.

Money didn't matter.

Love mattered.

Family mattered.

Oh, my God. Anna.

"Bless you," he said to Mrs. Burbridge. He raced down the hall to the door. He had to find Anna—now, at once.

He stopped short when he saw Cooper standing outside his door. The burly bodyguard's face was white and drawn.

"Boss—"

But at that moment Nikos saw the bundle in Cooper's arms. His baby son, wrapped in a blanket. Michael's little face was red and miserable as he cried.

"We found him at the front entrance to the casino," Cooper said. "Alone."

Nikos's heart stopped in his throat as he took his son in his arms. "Alone?"

The burly man nodded grimly. "A valet said a van stopped beneath the marquee, left the baby on the ground, and drove away."

Nikos held his son close, crooning to him softly, rocking him back and forth against his chest, just like Anna had taught him. The baby's tears subsided. Michael was comforted, but Nikos was not. "Anna wouldn't let herself be separated from Misha."

Looking miserable, Cooper handed him a letter. Nikos scanned it quickly.

Nikos

I've realized that sharing custody will never work. I'm in love with Victor Sinistyn and leaving with him for South America. You once said I was no kind of mother, and I guess you were right. Trying to keep our baby safe and warm would be too much effort where we're going. Please don't bother trying to find me. Raise our son well.
Anna

"Boss?" Cooper repeated unhappily. His voice echoed in the private outside hallway against the steel of the elevator doors. "What do you want me to do?"

Nikos's heart was pounding. She'd left him. The moment he'd realized he loved her with all his heart, she'd left him. His worst fear had come true.

But something nagged at him, overriding the pain, and he read the letter again. A mere hour after she'd left Nikos she'd decided to leave both him and Misha behind for a life with Victor Sinistyn?

Maybe it *was* her handwriting, but he didn't believe a word of it.

"She's in trouble," Nikos said slowly. "Someone forced her to write this letter."

"You think she's been kidnapped?"

"Sinistyn," he breathed. The man had made it clear he wanted Anna, and when Nikos had shoved her out of L'Hermitage without bodyguards he'd handed her to him on a silver plate. He cursed himself under his breath. "Get the plane ready."

"It's ready now—for your trip to Asia."

"Screw Singapore. Let Haverstock take the bid," he said, throwing away the billion-dollar deal to his chief rival without a thought.

"Where are we going to look for her? South America?"

Nikos shook his head. "Sinistyn put that in to throw us off the track. No. He's going someplace else. Somewhere private. Somewhere my power does not easily reach." He glanced down at the letter, forcing himself to read it again slowly.

You once said I was no kind of mother…
Trying to keep our baby safe and warm would
be too much effort where we're going…

He sucked in his breath. She was trying to tell him where they were going. Folding the letter, he shoved it at Cooper. "They're going to Russia."

"Let me guess, boss," Cooper said sourly. "You want to handle this alone."

Nikos gently handed the baby to Mrs. Burbridge. Kissing his son goodbye, he turned to face Cooper with rage surging through his veins. "Hell, no. I want every man we've got on the plane within the hour. And get Yuri Andropov on the phone. It's time to call in a favor."

CHAPTER NINE

ANNA shifted slightly in her chair, trying to shift the cords that bound her wrists without attracting the attention of Victor or his goons. Her hands felt hot and sweaty with the effort, but the rest of her felt like ice as she worked the broken tines of her great-grandmother's ring against the rope.

On the car ride from St. Petersburg she'd briefly felt the spring sun on her face, but the backroom of the Rostov Palace felt cold as ever. Especially as she'd listened to Victor's men ransack the Princess's china in the kitchen. Biting her lip, she watched as Victor and one of his men set up an old black-and-white television near the fire.

"It's not working. We'll miss the game," the bodyguard complained in Russian, trying to position the antenna.

"It'll be fine," Victor snapped in the same language. He took the antenna then, realizing that there was no electricity, dropped it in disgust. "Go help with dinner."

"Why can't *she* make us dinner?" the man grumbled, nodding at Anna. "Make the woman useful for once."

Victor glanced back at her, and she froze.

"Oh, she will be useful. But only to me. Get out, I said. I want some time with my future bride."

As Victor approached she pressed her wrists against her T-shirt, hoping he wouldn't notice that one of the cords binding her to the chair was finally starting to fray.

She'd been praying that customs officials would discover her when they arrived in St. Petersburg, but Victor's connections, along with a well-placed bribe, had allowed his private plane to arrive unmolested.

At least her baby was safe, thousands of miles away with Nikos. She'd bought her child's safety with that horrible letter Victor had forced her to write. Would Nikos see her clues?

Maybe he won't even care, she thought hollowly. He'd made it clear that he wanted her permanently out of his life, and this was about as permanent as it could get.

Victor pulled off her gag. "Here," he said, sounding amused. "Scream all you want. No one will hear you."

But she didn't scream. She just pulled away from his touch, glaring at him.

He laughed, folding his arms as he looked around them. "I can see I need to renovate my so-called palace. No heat. No electricity. And all they've found in the kitchen so far are potatoes and teabags."

"I hope you starve," she replied pleasantly.

"That's not a very kind thing to say to your future husband, is it? You and I both need to keep up our strength. I'll send one of the boys to the grocery store. And as for heat…we can supply that on our own, later."

He gave her a sly smile. "Any requests? You've been refusing food and drink for hours." He ran his hand down her arm, making her shudder with revulsion. "You must eat something."

"So you can drug me? No thanks."

"Ah, *loobemaya*," Victor said softly, brushing back a tendril of her hair. "I wouldn't go to so much trouble if I didn't love you so much."

"You call this love?"

"Until Stavrakis's spell wears off, and you understand it's really me you want, I need to keep you close. You will realize how much you want me." His voice sounded threatening as, massaging her shoulder hard enough to leave a bruise, he added softly, "Very soon."

Ignoring the loud sounds of crashing china and slamming cabinet doors in the kitchen, Anna pulled her shoulder away from his hand. "I love Nikos, and I always will."

He yanked back her hair, causing her head to jerk back. Anna dimly heard men shouting from the kitchen, but all she could see was Victor's sadistic face, inches away from her own. "Forget him. Forget his baby. I will give you others. I will fill you with my child tonight. You belong to me now. You will learn to obey my will. You will learn to crave my touch—"

He forced his lips on hers in a painful ravishment that was meant to teach fear. And it worked. For the first time Anna began to feel truly scared of what he would do to her.

When he pulled away, Victor smiled at the expression on her face. He ran a hand up the inner thigh of her jeans.

"You have no right," she whispered, shaking.

"This is my country. I have half the police in my pocket. Here, you are my slave." He reached to fondle a breast, and without thinking she brought up her bound wrists to block him. His smile stretched to a grin. "Yes," he breathed. "Fight me. That's what I want. Stavrakis isn't here to save you. You'll never see him or your precious son again. You're mine. You're totally in my power—"

"Let her go."

Victor looked up with a gasp. Anna saw Nikos standing in the kitchen doorway and almost sobbed aloud.

Nikos's face had an expression she'd never seen before—as cold and deadly as the gun he was pointing at Sinistyn.

Victor looked up with an intake of breath which he quickly masked with a sneer. "You're as good as dead, Stavrakis. My men will—"

"Your men will do nothing. They barely tried. When they saw they were outnumbered, most of them gave up without a fight." He cocked the gun, assessing his aim at Victor's head. "Some loyalty you inspire, Sinistyn."

With a single smooth movement Victor twisted behind Anna, using her body to block his own. "Come closer and I'll kill her."

He put his beefy hands around her neck. Anna flinched, then struggled, unable to breathe. As he slowly tightened his grip, the room around her seemed to shimmer and fade.

Nikos uncocked the gun, pointing it at the ceiling. "You really are a coward."

"It's easy to throw insults when you have a gun."

"Let her go, damn you!" Nikos threw the gun on the floor, then straightened with a scornful expression. "Even now I'm unarmed, I know you won't fight me. I'm stronger, faster, smarter than you—"

"Shut up!" Victor screamed, releasing Anna's throat. She took a long, shuddering gasp of air and felt the world right itself around her.

Victor stormed toward Nikos, lunging for the gun.

Nikos kicked it into the roaring fireplace and threw himself at the other man's midsection. The two men fought while Anna watched in terror, desperately struggling with the cords that bound her to the chair. Victor lashed out wildly, hitting Nikos's jaw with his knee. Nikos's head snapped back, but he fought grimly, as if he were in the battle he'd trained for all his life. With a crunching uppercut to the chin, Nikos knocked Victor to the floor.

Gasping for air, Victor slid back, scuttling like a crab. Reaching into the fireplace, he picked up the gun with his sleeve and pushed himself up against the wall, panting.

"Now you're going to die." Victor shot a crazed look from Nikos to Anna. "And you're going to watch. After this, only his ghost will haunt us." He cocked the gun, pointing it at Nikos with triumph.

"No!" Anna screamed, desperately struggling with the cord. By some miracle it snapped open against her wrist. She threw herself from the chair, flinging her body in front of Nikos as Victor squeezed the trigger.

She closed her eyes, waiting to feel the bullet tear through her body.

Instead, she just heard a soft *click*.

The gun was empty!

Victor shook the gun with impotent fury.

Nikos turned to one side, tucking her protectively behind him as he faced Victor. "Guess I forgot the bullets. Sorry."

With a scream of frustration Victor threw the gun at him, but Nikos dodged it easily. It clattered to the floor.

Nikos glanced at it with a derisive snort. He raised an eyebrow, giving Victor the darkly arrogant look that Anna had once despised. But she appreciated it now. She knew he used all his arrogance, all his strength and power, to protect the people he loved.

"Fight me, Sinistyn," Nikos demanded coldly. "Just you and me."

Victor swore in Russian, shaking his head. He looked straight at Anna, muttering all the sadistic things he'd do to her if Nikos wasn't there to protect her.

Anna felt her cheeks grow hot with horror. Nikos didn't speak Russian, but when he saw the effect the man's words were having on her he strode forward grimly.

With a yelp, Victor turned and ran in the other direction. But Nikos caught up with him, grabbing his shoulder and whirling him around.

"Like scaring women, do you?" He punched Victor in the face—once, twice. "Too much of a coward to fight someone your own size? Fight me, damn you! Or are you going to just let me kill you?" Nikos's eyes narrowed and he looked dangerous indeed. "Don't think I won't."

Victor started fighting dirty. He tried to knee Nikos in the groin, to trip him. When Nikos blocked him, he stumbled back to the fireplace and grabbed a sharp iron poker.

"I'll stab you like a pig, you Greek bastard," he panted, swinging the poker at Nikos's face.

He blocked it with his right arm, but Anna heard the crunch of bone and saw the way Nikos's right hand hung at a strange angle.

Victor had broken his wrist. She trembled with fury. She started to run at Victor, to fight him two to one, but Nikos stopped her with a hard glance.

With his left hand he wrenched the poker away and threw Victor to the floor. He held him to the ground with one hand against his neck. Anna watched in horror as he tightened his grip.

"How does it feel to be vulnerable?" Nikos demanded.

"Nikos, let him go," Anna sobbed.

"Why? Do you think he would have let *you* go?" he demanded, not looking at her. "Did he ever show mercy to anyone weaker? Why should I let him live after what he's done to you?"

Slowly she put her hands against his shoulders, feeling the hard tension of his muscles. "Do it for us. Please, my love, let him go so we can go back to our son."

Abruptly, he released his choke-hold on the other man and rose to his feet. She had one brief vision of his face, and she thought she saw tears in his eyes as, without a word, he took her in his arms and held her tightly.

Nikos looked down at her as he held her tenderly to his chest. His dark eyes were shining.

"Thank you, *agape mou*," he whispered, brushing her cheek softly with his hand. "Thank you for trying to take that bullet. There weren't any bullets, but you didn't know that. You…you saved me. In so many ways."

"And you started early," a man said from the doorway in heavily accented English. Anna looked up to see a man in a Russian police uniform, with half a dozen policemen behind him. "We missed it."

"I couldn't wait, Yuri." Nikos jerked his head toward Victor, still stretched out on the floor. "There he is."

The man called Yuri smiled. "You said you were calling in a favor. I wish I had to pay more favors like this. We've wanted Sinistyn a long time, but he was untouchable. Now, with your testimony and influence, he won't see the sun again for a long time." The policeman looked with concern at Nikos's wrist. "My friend, you are hurt."

"It's nothing—"

"It's his wrist. I think it's broken. We need a doctor right away," Anna said, then looked up anxiously at the face of the man she loved. "Please, Nikos. I need you to be well."

"All right," he muttered. "Get the doctor."

Turning away from the policeman, he sank into a

nearby chair and pulled her into his lap. "Anna, before the doctor starts filling me with drugs, I have to tell you something. I should have told you this a long time ago, but I was too stupid to see it and too stubborn to admit it—even to myself. I really do love you."

"Nikos, I love—"

"Please let me finish, while I can still get this out." He took a deep breath. "You saved me. From a life that was empty. I was stupid to prevent you from working, or doing anything else that brings you joy. If it makes you happy, I want you to work. As my secretary, as vice-president, as any damn thing you want."

Tears filled her eyes even as she gave him a mischievous smile. "I think I'd make a good CEO."

"Cocky." He returned her grin. "You always were the only one who could stand up to me. I need that in my life. Someone to keep me in my place."

As she looked into his handsome face she barely heard the noises of the swarming police, or Victor's whining complaints as they took him away.

"Your place is with me." She cupped his jaw, rough with dark stubble, in her hands. "As long as we're together, anyplace in the world is my home. But there's something that I have to ask you. Something I've never said before to anyone." He'd called her cocky, but what she wanted to ask him now terrified her. She took a deep breath. "Nikos, will you marry me?"

For answer, his smile lit his face from within, his dark eyes shining at her with hope and love. "I thought you'd never ask."

* * *

"I told you we should have gotten married at the drive-thru chapel in Vegas," Anna whispered when she reached the end of the aisle.

"And miss all this? Never," he whispered back with a wink.

As the priest began to speak the words that would bind them together for all time Nikos knew he should pay attention, but all he could do was look at his bride. Beneath the hot Greek sun, on the edge of a rocky cliff overlooking the Aegean Sea, they were surrounded by flowers and a small audience of people who loved them. It was a simple wedding, plain by some standards, but he knew in his heart it was what Anna wanted.

And, looking at her now, he knew he'd never be able to deny her anything. Her turquoise eyes, a mixture of sea and sky, smiled at him as he lifted her veil. She wore a white shift that made her look like a medieval maiden.

Her engagement ring, a four-carat diamond in an antique gold setting, sparkled from her finger. He'd given it to her two nights ago. She'd tried to refuse it until she'd realized that he'd found the original stone from her great-grandmother's wedding ring. Now it was one of her greatest treasures.

The way she'd thanked him had made him forget all about the cast on his wrist. Remembering that night, and every night since they'd returned from Russia, still made his body feel hot from the inside out. He could hardly wait to give Anna her honeymoon present—Rostov Palace, which he'd bought from Sinistyn's confiscated estates. Sinistyn didn't need it anymore, as he'd be living out his days in a Russian prison.

Nikos glanced around him at family and friends and the sea and the bright blue sky. *Justice.* Another thing he'd thought existed only in fairytales, along with love and happy endings.

He'd not only held his wedding in his parents' hometown, but, at Anna's urging, he'd invited his father's family—Eudocia Dounas and her three daughters—to the wedding. To his surprise they'd all come, bringing their husbands and children. He now had a family. Siblings, nieces, nephews. He didn't know them yet, but he would.

Near his family sat Anna's mother who, in another wedding-day miracle, was not only on her best behavior, but had pinched his cheek and declared it was "about time" the two were married. Anna had spent last night talking to her sister, barring Nikos from her bedroom because it was "bad luck" for him to see her. Now, Natalie was bouncing Misha on her knee while she watched the wedding, smiling through her tears. And he could see his son's two new top teeth in his smile as he watched his parents wed.

It was a day for families to join together.

All right, he'd admit it. It wasn't just Anna who'd wanted this kind of wedding. He had wanted it as well. In some way he'd wanted this all his life.

Family.

Home.

Love.

As Anna said the words that made her his wife her voice was sweet and true. He barely remembered repeating the words himself, but he must have done so since before he knew it the priest was speaking in accented English, declaring them husband and wife, and he was kissing the bride. Over the sound of the crashing surf he heard their family and friends behind them burst into applause, and a noisy cheer from Cooper. But as he kissed her, holding her tightly in his arms, all he could feel was the pounding of his heart against hers.

She pulled back, caressing his face as she grinned up at him through tears. "See?" she whispered. "Wasn't that better than having Elvis marry us?"

Hiding a grin, he looked down at her solemnly. "I'm yours to command now, Mrs. Stavrakis."

"Mine to command?" She paused, pretending to consider her options, and then leaned forward to whisper in his ear. "In that case, my first order is that you take me to bed."

"Leaving our guests to start the reception?"

She gave him a wicked smile. "They won't miss us."

"They won't even notice," he agreed with a grin. He picked her up in his arms and, to the delighted gasps of the crowd, he turned to carry her back to his villa.

"Ah, Anna. I can tell I'm going to have a hard life with you," he observed with a sigh, and he kissed her with all his heart.

MILLS & BOON
MODERN
Extra

On sale 7th September 2007

STEAMY SURRENDER
by Ally Blake

Morgan had come from Paris to see her inheritance
for herself – a row of shops in a Melbourne suburb.
Their spokesman was millionaire gelateria owner
Saxon Ciantar, and he made certain she knew where she
stood: she was their evil landlady and they were at war!
But Saxon soon began to see glimpses of the real Morgan
– and then he decided that he would fast-thaw the
ice maiden with his searing touch!

DREAM JOB, HOT BOSS!
by Robyn Grady

Working in Sydney's most dynamic advertising agency,
Serena Stevens is in heaven! And she's just landed the
agency's biggest account – this will make or break her
career… Serena's sexy boss, Australia's top tycoon
David Miles, may be all business in the boardroom,
but soon he is loosening his tie…and he wants a little
business in the bedroom! Before long Serena has
to choose…her dream job versus her hot boss!

MILLS & BOON
MODERN™
On sale 7th September 2007

THE MEDITERRANEAN BILLIONAIRE'S SECRET BABY
by Diana Hamilton

Francesco Mastroianni's affair with Anna was cut short when her father tried to blackmail Francesco. Seven months later, he is shocked to see Anna – struggling to make ends meet and visibly pregnant!

THE BOSS'S WIFE FOR A WEEK
by Anne McAllister

Spence Tyack needed a wife for a week… It seemed his demure personal assistant Sadie would take the role – and not only was she sensible in the boardroom, she was sensual in the bedroom!

THE KOUROS MARRIAGE REVENGE
by Abby Green

Kallie knew love had nothing to do with her marriage to Alexandros Kouros. Alex would have revenge for the mistake that had shattered both their pasts when he took her as his arranged bride…

JED HUNTER'S RELUCTANT BRIDE
by Susanne James

When wealthy Jed Hunter offers Cryssie a job as his assistant, she has to take it: she has a sick sister to provide for. Soon Jed demands Cryssie marry him – it makes good business sense. But Cryssie's feelings run deeper…

Available at WHSmith, Tesco, ASDA, and all good bookshops
www.millsandboon.co.uk

FREE

4 BOOKS AND A SURPRISE GIFT!

We would like to take this opportunity to thank you for reading this Mills & Boon® book by offering you the chance to take FOUR more specially selected titles from the Modern™ series absolutely FREE! We're also making this offer to introduce you to the benefits of the Mills & Boon® Reader Service™—

- ★ FREE home delivery
- ★ FREE gifts and competitions
- ★ FREE monthly Newsletter
- ★ Books available before they're in the shops
- ★ Exclusive Reader Service offers

Accepting these FREE books and gift places you under no obligation to buy; you may cancel at any time, even after receiving your free shipment. Simply complete your details below and return the entire page to the address below. You don't even need a stamp!

YES! Please send me 4 free Modern books and a surprise gift. I understand that unless you hear from me, I will receive 6 superb new titles every month for just £2.89 each, postage and packing free. I am under no obligation to purchase any books and may cancel my subscription at any time. The free books and gift will be mine to keep in any case.

P7ZEE

Ms/Mrs/Miss/Mr.........................Initials ....
BLOCK CAPITALS PLEASE

Surname ....

Address ....

....

....Postcode ....

Send this whole page to:
The Reader Service, FREEPOST CN81, Croydon, CR9 3WZ.